TEN
DAYS

BOOKS BY MEL SHERRATT

DETECTIVE EDEN BERRISFORD CRIME THRILLER SERIES
The Girls Next Door
Don't Look Behind You

THE ESTATE SERIES
Somewhere to Hide
Behind a Closed Door
Fighting for Survival
Written in the Scars

THE DS GRACE ALLENDALE SERIES
Hush Hush
Tick Tock
Liar Liar
Good Girl

THE DETECTIVE ALLIE SHENTON SERIES
Taunting the Dead
Follow the Leader
Only the Brave You

The Lies You Tell
Watching Over You

WRITING AS MARCIE STEELE
Stirred with Love
Secrets, Lies & Love
Second Chances at Love
The Man Across the Street
Coming Home to Hope Street

TEN DAYS

MEL SHERRATT

bookouture

Published by Bookouture in 2021

An imprint of Storyfire Ltd.
Carmelite House
50 Victoria Embankment
London EC4Y 0DZ

www.bookouture.com

ISBN: 978-1-80019-527-1
eBook ISBN: 978-1-80019-526-4

Previously published as *Invisible Victim*

2006

The room is almost in darkness. The smell of pee fills my nostrils and I turn my nose up in disgust. I try to think of something else but it isn't easy. I look down at him, lying still next to me. My arm is around his shoulder, and he clings to my body. I don't know what else to do.

His eyes are closed.

'Wake up.' I prod him in the shoulder.

When he doesn't respond, my heart starts beating like a drum. It's so loud in my ears that I think I might blow up.

'Wake up. Wake up!'

There is no reply but I will not cry.

He finally speaks. His voice is almost a whisper.

'I'm cold,' he says.

I laugh because I'm so relieved. But it isn't long before I feel him going floppy in my arms again.

'You have to stay awake until the morning,' I encourage. 'You'll feel better by then.'

'Tired.'

My stomach rumbles, and I hear a faint giggle from him. He's still with me – is that a good sign?

'Shall we play a game?' I urge. 'I spy?'

'So cold.'

I pull him in closer to keep him warm.

I must have fallen asleep, because when I wake, it's completely dark and I am scared. I speak to him again but he's so quiet.

And I know.

I sit and I cry. I don't know what to do now I'm on my own. I have all night to worry about it because no one will come to me, no matter how loud I scream.

They will have to let me out soon. There will be trouble because of what's happened to him. And once I get out of here, things are going to be different.

Because I might only be ten years old, but I have had enough.

And taking him away from me changes everything.

DAY 1

13 August 2019

CHAPTER ONE

Eva

Eva Farmer raced into the kitchen, her eyes flicking around every surface. Only last night, she and her husband, Nick, had downed a glass of wine at the celebratory news that he'd passed his sergeant's exam. Nick had been a police officer for the past ten years. With his shift work, they flitted around each other most of the time. So the wine had been a joy to share, as well as the film they'd watched, and the fun they'd had afterwards. It was good to connect whenever they could.

As usual, Eva was looking for her car keys.

'Have you seen my…?'

Nick was sitting at the breakfast bar. He pointed to the worktop with his spoon as he crunched on his cereal. Already he was dressed for work. Even now, ten years after they were married, Eva wasn't sure if it was the uniform or the man wearing it that first made her heart skip a beat. He'd been with her through everything, more recently when Daniel had started to pester her to meet. Several times, he'd turned up outside the *Stoke News* office where she'd worked since leaving university. She'd refused to have anything to do with him and, in the end, she'd had to get Nick to give him a subtle warning.

What she hadn't told Nick was that several times recently. As she'd stepped out lunch break. After a visit to the gym. Once when out of a meeting in town. Her rationale was the longer him, the quicker he would get the message. She didn't wa him – not after what had happened.

She sighed. How had she managed to put her keys in the fruit bowl again? It was never her phone: that went everywhere with her. Her job meant she had to be in touch constantly. Still, at thirty-three, it gave her a buzz for adventure that distracted her from the fact that she and Nick had been trying to conceive for the past year.

She patted Nick on the shoulder as she rushed past. 'What time are you finishing this evening?'

'About eight-ish.'

'I'll get something nice for supper.' She picked up her keys and grinned at him. 'I enjoyed last night. I wish we got to do it more often.'

Nick was two years older than Eva. They'd been together since they were in their early twenties, marrying four years later. He stood nearly a foot taller than her, at six foot three, and could chuck her over his shoulder as if she weighed the same as a bag of sugar. As well as lifting and pushing ridiculously heavy weights, he ran several times a week. Add to that a cheeky grin, short black hair with an undercut and Eva had everything she'd ever wanted right there.

Nick reached for her as she went past, pulling her close to kiss her.

'You taste of milk,' she teased.

'You taste of ecstasy.' He grinned.

'If I didn't know you better, I'd say you were offering me a compliment there, but as you see what drugs do to people every day…'

h, can you get me a card
week? You know we're due

his embrace and went to fill
'

ns into the air and stretched.
day?'

ning and then it's mostly office

ys
he'd seen Daniel again,
o the shops on her
he was coming
she ignored
t to see

9

There   besides Eva in her section, all of
whom covered genera...   senior features editor, she'd been
delegating work for four years. Selfishly, she kept the good jobs
for herself, but then it was a case of hierarchy. Out of them, she'd
been the longest serving at the *Stoke News*, remaining loyal to
the newspaper. Or rather she enjoyed the job so much, she didn't
want to leave.

Eva had never been one to glorify or sensationalise others' bad
news. Her idea of news telling was to dwell on the positive as
much as possible. There was enough crap in the world without
her getting normal people to bear their soul for all to read about,
and then twisting it even further for reader enjoyment. She liked
to add her name with pride to articles she wrote. She would never
deviate from that either.

'Let's hope not,' Nick said. 'It isn't often I get to do the day
shift. I intend to make the most of the next four evenings too.'

Half an hour later, they said their goodbyes. Eva was last to
leave, glancing up at the house before reversing out of the driveway.
Their home really was their castle, despite long hours away from
it. They were the epitome of a newer class – small, detached home
on a pleasant private housing estate; two almost-new cars; and
two higher-than-average salaries coming in every month. They
shopped where they liked, holidayed overseas twice a year and
went out as often as they could get together. Having been raised

in a tower block, Eva knew she was lucky to live the way she did now. Things could easily have been very different.

Eva was meeting a property developer at a warehouse he'd recently purchased, to chat about a new business venture. She wrote a quick message to her PA to tell her she was going straight out on-site, rather than calling into the office first, and would be back around midday. If she wasn't long, she'd buy cakes on the way back.

CHAPTER TWO

Eva

Eva was having trouble rousing herself. The pain in her head intensified and she reached a hand up to her temple, wincing. It was painful and swollen to the touch. Slowly she opened her eyes.

She frowned as she failed to recognise her surroundings, then flinched again with the effort. She squinted until her vision adjusted to the dim light. Was it night-time? Her hand shot to her ribs and she groaned in pain. They too felt bruised.

She reached a hand out to her bedside cabinet, to locate her phone. But it wasn't there. Neither was her bedside cabinet. All she was met with was a wall.

Sitting up in a panic, her breathing became shallow as she took in her surroundings. What had happened to her? She tried to think back but she couldn't remember anything. She couldn't even recall what day of the week it was. Was it morning or evening?

The room was tiny: no bigger than a large shed. She looked closer to see there was exposed brickwork. The ceiling was low, with beams that supported the floor above. A whiff of damp permeated the musty air.

With her left hand, she covered the swollen eye that was still refusing to completely open and concentrated on looking through the other one. She was sitting on a mattress, one sheet and a tiny pillow atop it. In front was a small window, too high for her to look through, unless she pulled herself up the wall. It was narrow, perhaps twenty centimetres wide and roughly a metre high. There was no handle she could see, and the glass was opaque with wire meshing embedded inside.

Fear ripped through her the more she noticed. Her watch was gone. Her wedding ring was missing too. Her hand touched the space where her necklace would have been. Missing.

She looked down at her clothes. The grey sweatshirt and jogging bottoms didn't belong to her: why was she wearing them? Her feet were bare, red toenails prominent. She couldn't see her boots anywhere. In the far corner, there was a bucket: the only other item in the room except for the mattress.

She sat quietly, seeing if she could hear any noise, but there was nothing. The room reminded her of her gran's cellar in the terraced house she'd lived in before she'd died. Eva remembered it as a place she'd loved and hated. It had been down a few steps and then underneath the house. Dark and full of dust and rubbish – and spiders. Just the thought made her waft a hand around her head at imaginary legs crawling all over her.

Ignoring the pain in her head, she turned around swiftly and put her feet to the floor. There was a wooden door to her right. Slowly she stood up and walked towards it, taking tentative steps on the cold tiles. As she reached it, she saw there was no handle.

Gasping for breath, she banged on the door.

'Hello?'

It was then she noticed the hole cut away in the bottom panel. Even before stooping down to examine it, tears pricked her eyes. Because realisation was dawning on her. There was a pet flap fitted, the flap itself removed to leave a hole. But behind it was a piece of wood that covered it. Even if she could kick it away, it wasn't big enough for her to climb through.

Which is what the first woman to be abducted had told her. And the second. And the third.

Over the past few months, Eva had been working on a feature involving three women who had been kidnapped and released after ten days. There was a fourth woman who had gone missing too, but she hadn't come home at all. The police were working on all cases but, in particular, woman number four, Jillian Bradshaw, a serving police officer and a friend of hers and Nick's. She'd gone missing four weeks ago. With a fresh police appeal, Eva had been asked by her boss to compile a four-page spread on the women, to garner public interest again.

'Is anyone there?' she shouted, banging on the door with the side of her fists. 'Hello! Let me out. Please! Is anyone there?'

She made as much noise as possible, until her hands hurt too much to continue. Crying, she slid down the wall and sat on the floor. Ignoring the pain in her ribs, she pulled in her knees and tucked her arms around them. She shivered, whether through cold or shock she wasn't sure.

Eva started to think. How had she got here? Who had she met today? Or yesterday? What day was it? Where had she been going? Try as she might, she couldn't recall any details.

A rush of nausea flooded through her and she only just reached the bucket in time to throw up. Wiping her mouth with her sleeve afterwards, she burst into tears again. She couldn't deny the truth any longer.

She was the fifth woman to be abducted.

JANUARY 2019

CHAPTER THREE

Stoke News

Woman Missing for Two Days
Eva Farmer, Senior News Reporter
12 January 2019

Staffordshire Police are looking into the disappearance of local woman, Stephanie Harvey, 36. Mrs Harvey, who lives in Werrington, Stoke-on-Trent, was last seen by her husband on her way to attend a morning training seminar in Shelton.

CCTV footage has shown Mrs Harvey in her vehicle. She was last seen walking along College Road at 9.15 a.m. on Friday, 10 January. Her car has since been removed from the college car park.

Mrs Harvey is married, with twin boys aged seven. The police were alerted by her husband when she failed to collect them from school in the afternoon as she usually does.

Michael Harvey, 39, says it is unlike his wife to be gone for so long without contact, even more so not to collect the boys. 'She wouldn't go anywhere without ringing or texting me to arrange for someone else to pick them up instead.

'We're not in any financial difficulties and she wasn't anxious or depressed. We'd been booking our summer holidays online at the weekend. This isn't like her. I'm really worried.'

DCI Stan Hedley, Senior Investigating Officer, said they were reaching out to the general public to try and jog memories.

'Mrs Harvey hasn't used her phone, nor been in contact with her family or friends,' he commented. 'We urge everyone to think back to what they were doing around the time she went missing, and to contact us if they can recollect anything, no matter how trivial, and get in touch with us on the helpline printed below.'

CHAPTER FOUR

Eva

Eva turned her car into Carlton Avenue, located number nine and parked outside. She glanced at the house and its surroundings. It was a pleasant street, the proverbial tree-lined suburban retreat, where identical houses stood in a line either side.

The Harvey family knew she was coming. As usual, she felt excited by the feature she was putting together, though she would be sensitive to the family's needs. Charlie Peterson, the editor-in-chief, had known Eva since she'd started as a junior reporter when she was twenty and had given the gig to her.

A man came to the door, a woman close behind him: Stephanie and Mike Harvey.

'Hello,' Eva said, introducing herself.

'Please come in.' Stephanie beckoned her forward. The hall was small with the three of them standing in it. Eva followed them through a door on their right.

The living room was a perfect scene of domestic bliss: a far cry from where Stephanie had been held for ten days. It was decorated in pale grey and white striped wallpaper. Two three-seater sofas were set out in an L-shape around a pine coffee table, with a blue rug underneath. Above an Adams-style fireplace was a portrait of the family. Stephanie used to have long red hair, teased into curls that almost touched the floor. She sat cross-legged with two little boys in front of her, Mike at her side. They were all laughing, natural and a joy to see. It was a beautiful portrait, bringing an immediate pang of sadness to her.

'Would you like a drink?' Mike offered.

'Coffee would be great, please.' Eva nodded and sat down with Stephanie. The back half of the room opened up into a conservatory. There were piles of toys in colourful plastic boxes and a train track laid out on the floor. The walls were covered in more photos of the boys: identical twins.

Eva took out her notebook. Often, she'd record a conversation when she was reporting on a story, but for this she was going old school. She'd learned shorthand in college: one of the best skills she'd gained before she took a degree in journalism.

She stole a quick look at Stephanie. Her hair was now cut in a chic pixie style that suited her oval face.

'How are you doing?' Eva asked. 'Stupid question, I know.'

'So-so. I want to get on with my life, but it's hard.'

'I can't begin to imagine.'

'What is it that you'd like to know?'

'As I mentioned on the phone, I'm compiling a feature, if you're comfortable with that? I think, too, the public need to know why they should stay vigilant.'

'We've been through this with the police,' Mike said, his tone a little sharp as he rejoined them, placing three mugs on the coffee table.

Stephanie rested a hand on his arm. 'He's concerned about me dredging it all up again,' she explained. 'I want this story told properly, and I know you'll do a good job. A sensitive one. And besides, he's still out there.' She turned back to Eva.

Mike snorted in disdain. Eva saw Stephanie throw him a cautionary look. He sat back in his chair with a sigh.

'Would you like me to recap for you?' Stephanie asked Eva.

Eva nodded. Although she had all of those details in her notes, she wanted to encourage Stephanie to talk.

'The room I was kept in was dark with one narrow window that let me know whether it was day or night. It was a godsend at first, but then I forgot whether I'd been there for five days or six. After that, I lost count and until I was told it was ten days after my release, I didn't have a clue.'

'And no one spoke to you at all?'

Stephanie shook her head.

Eva wondered how she'd react to having her own hair cut off, among the other degrading things that had happened to Stephanie when she was held captive. Eva would have been devastated to lose all those beautiful waves. And it was a cruel trick. Was it to make Stephanie seem a shadow of her former self? Was that what the kidnapper wanted her to be?

'I was beaten up before I was locked in the room, my wounds left unattended,' Stephanie went on. 'I wasn't let out to wash or use the bathroom. There was a bucket in the corner of the room.' Her eyes dropped to the floor in embarrassment, but then she looked straight into Eva's eyes. 'I was given hardly any food. There was nothing to wash with. I stank when I came out. And I was naked.'

Even though Eva knew a lot of these details, the hairs on her body stood on end as she listened to Stephanie recount her ordeal. What had happened to her was barbaric, way beyond a joke if someone was out to seek revenge.

It would be Eva's worst nightmare, being locked in a room for ten days. She was a chatterbox and needed her phone like it was a drug to keep her alive. She wouldn't be able to cope as a prisoner.

And yet there seemed to be no reason why Stephanie had been chosen. Eva went through Stephanie's history with her, but there was nothing else she could tease out because there wasn't anything to tell. Stephanie Harvey seemed to be in the wrong place at the wrong time. When Stephanie was let out after ten days, the mystery deepened: it was so unusual for anyone to be released – especially if it could lead to an arrest and conviction.

'I still don't know why he singled me out,' Stephanie went on. 'I'm just a normal person. I've done no harm to anyone. I've only had three jobs all my life – a support worker at a charity for teenagers, a few years in an office doing accounts and then again at an insurance brokers. I finished the last position because I was ill with cancer. But now I've had the all-clear, I've recently gone back to university to study psychology.'

Eva watched Stephanie reach up to her neck. During her captivity and while under the influence of drugs, she had been tattooed with the number one. Stephanie had covered it with four intertwined hearts in black ink. It might look better now but, equally, Eva assumed it would always serve as a reminder of those harrowing days. Every time Stephanie saw it, she would know what lay underneath.

Eva knew Nick and the team had been doing their best to find the kidnapper, but without any details of where Stephanie had been held and then her being returned to where she had last been seen, it would be hard to piece together. It was clear, however, that someone knew Stoke well, knew how to stay invisible and under the radar.

'And after he let you go?' Eva went on.

'I was dropped off in the middle of the night, in a street where there was limited CCTV.'

'And you're sure you have no idea who it would be?'

'I think that's enough,' Mike said, getting to his feet. 'I don't like what you're insinuating, that my wife must have done something wrong for this to have happened.'

'I'm sorry. I didn't mean to imply that at all. I live and breathe stories but I never embellish anything. I think it's a disservice to you if I don't tell the truth. And we're not a national paper. We serve the local community. My articles are always sensitive, I can assure you of that.'

'It's okay, Mike,' Stephanie insisted.

Eva thought about her visit later that afternoon when she sat down to write the piece. It would be run in the newspaper and online the following day. The photographer had been to take more photos: Stephanie and Mike sitting on the settee, hand in hand. Eva had stared at it for a while, still unable to contemplate how they must be feeling.

She began to write with a hint of sadness. Someone's wife and mother had been abducted and, even since Stephanie's return, there was no denying things would have changed for everyone involved. Luckily, the Harveys' marriage seemed strong enough to get them through the ordeal. Understandably, Mike was very protective towards Stephanie and it was good to see.

As the wife of a police officer, Eva worried about Nick every day. She didn't know how she'd cope if he went out one morning and never came home. She shook away her melancholy thoughts and got to work again.

DAY 1

13 August 2019

CHAPTER FIVE

Alex

It's been quite exciting to think that Eva is in my cellar. Locked away from the world she knows, just for my enjoyment.

I make her a sandwich. I hope she likes cheese. I add a bit of lettuce for garnish. It's on white bread, the cheapest I could find. Then I make a drink of tea in a paper cup she can do no harm with, and pop it on a tray.

I'm so used to doing this now that I do it without fault. With each woman I've abducted, I have a set routine that they learn quickly enough. If she asks me for something, I won't answer, but I might take it down with me on the next visit, or the one after that. It will help her to stay focused, on her toes so to speak. After all, she has to keep her spirits up for the next ten days.

I can see her on the camera monitor. It's almost tea time: she's been down there for six hours now, since I left her on the mattress.

I wonder if she's still out for the count? The effects of the drugs should be wearing off soon. Perhaps if she hears me upstairs, she might start checking everything out. Or maybe she has already and I missed it.

I like this part best. The not knowing exactly how it's going to turn out. Although I'm very much in charge, it's down to Eva ultimately. I hope she's a good girl for me. If she isn't, I will become very, very cross. And she doesn't want that, now, does she?

The place I've rented, not in my name, of course, has been perfect for what I had in mind. An end town house with a tiny driveway that leads to a single garage. I never use my car unless I'm transporting the women. I bet half the people in my street don't even know I have one.

The cellar was the biggest draw to this property. I thought at first that I'd need to use a bedroom to keep the women trapped. But when the estate agent showed me the space downstairs, converted into a separate room, dark and damp with no access to the outside world and a door from the kitchen, I signed the paperwork as fast as I could. The cat flap I fitted myself, making it into a hatch. I'm quite proud of it actually. I'm usually useless at DIY.

It isn't a nice area to live in but it's good enough for my needs. The lease is for twelve months, but I'll be gone before it ends, one way or another.

The house next door was empty for the first three months, so I'd had the end of the street almost to myself. There's a field beside me, leading to a park and then onto the main road. I can hear the drone of the traffic but it doesn't bother me now.

I keep to myself but I'm a good neighbour. I take the bins out; I tidy the tiny scrap of garden out front. I have my food delivered for the most part. To all intents and purposes I am a model tenant.

Little do my neighbours know what notoriety I will be bringing to the area once everything comes out.

The women have been lucid and pliable for the most part. They just looked like they were drunk, or feeling unwell, and that I was taking care of them. Once I had them in the car, it was easy to get them into the house.

I slide across the bolt on the door leading to the cellar and open it. I listen, but there is no noise. Again I wonder if she's still out for the count, or just being quiet. Of course, I won't ask how she is. That's part of the plan too, you see. Not to speak to Eva. So she feels totally alone, completely invisible.

Just like I was for all those years.

I pick up the tray and go downstairs. My trainers tread lightly on the steps, almost like I'm sneaking up on Eva. The door is to my right. I kneel down, place the tray on the floor and open the hatch. I wish I could look inside to see where she is now. Who knows where she might be if she heard me coming down to her? I've been tricked this way before. Stephanie Harvey tried to kick me when I removed the lock from the hatch. But I'm not that stupid. She had no food for the rest of that day and the day after, for punishment.

Once the hatch is open, I use a grabber to slide the tray inside, holding on tightly to it in case she tries to reach for it. Alison Green did that. She almost got it off me, but I was quick to pull it back. Hurt my shoulder though, as she pulled so hard. That's when I had the idea of the grabber.

With every woman I've held captive, I've learned a little more about what not to do. I suppose it's always going to be a bit trial and error.

I've put a note on the tray. It reads:

PUSH EVERYTHING BACK THROUGH THE DOOR ONCE YOU'VE FINISHED WITH IT. NO FUNNY BUSINESS.

I listen again but there is no movement from inside the room.

I go back up the steps to monitor her, knowing if Eva looks through the hatch she can only see my feet. Then I close and lock the door behind me, making doubly sure I have locked it. I haven't ever forgotten but you never know. I don't want her to turn up unexpectedly in my kitchen.

I glance at the clock. It's almost time for my workout – it's a heavy weights session this evening. Good to rid myself of the pent-up energy I have. I always feel like this once I have another victim.

Alongside the food I need to pick up for my tea tomorrow, I make a mental note to bring Eva a newspaper. She won't be in today's editions because it will be too late.

But she'll definitely be headline news in the morning.

CHAPTER SIX

Alex and Milly

Milly is coming to tea this evening. I've been looking forward to it all day. It's nice to have someone to chat to, and Milly always makes me smile.

Milly is my only friend. I think back to when we met. I'd been watching her in the park for some time before I decided to approach her. She was a slight thing, always had her head down in a book. But I noticed something else about her: she reminded me of myself. That look she had about her. It said, 'Please don't come near me, as I don't want to interact with anyone, and yet I'm desperate for a friend.'

With the weather being breezy, she had her long blonde hair tucked into her coat to stop it from blowing across her face. Her woollen red scarf was wrapped tightly around her neck and looked cheap, possibly home-made. Her duffel coat seemed old-fashioned for someone in high school. Short flat shoes, black opaque tights and a skirt below her knee made me realise she was trying not to fit in any more.

I could recognise an invisible victim anywhere. That was the day I decided I would try and speak to her.

'Enjoying that?' I asked as I approached her.

She looked up with a start, glancing around to see who was nearby.

I held up my hand and I smiled. 'I've just finished it and wondered what you were thinking of it.'

She looked at me. 'It's good. I'm about halfway through.'

Before she could say anything, I sat down next to her. Not too close that I would frighten her; I knew I had to be careful. In fact, I was at the opposite end of the bench. She gave me a half-smile and then her head was in her book again.

I sat in silence for a minute or so.

'I love it here,' I said. 'I sit here often too. It's such a nice spot.' She nodded.

'You can see so much and yet still be on the edge. Sometimes I've seen you here and chosen another bench to sit on.'

'Oh! Sorry.' The girl gnawed at her bottom lip. 'I only usually come here after school during the week.'

'Well, I'd prefer to come when someone else is here. It's actually quite nice to talk. I live on my own.'

'I live with my mum,' she offered. And it was then that I knew I had her. Not wanting to overstay my welcome, I stood up.

'Well, I'll leave you to your reading. Nice meeting you…'

'Milly.'

'Nice meeting you, Milly. I'm Alex. See you.'

She smiled at me, and I smiled back before leaving. It *was* good to talk to someone. I wondered if she'd felt the same way. It seemed she did, as we then started meeting regularly.

Milly is a beautiful girl, pure and innocent looking. She's warm and kind. She's quite small and thin with a freckly face, bright blue eyes and full lips. If she had friends to help her style her hair, and apply make-up, she would be a looker. Not that I can help with either of those things, but she is a natural beauty.

Since meeting Milly, I've come out of my shell a little. Only with her, but it's been nice having a friend. We've gone to the cinema a couple of times, and she's visited my home several times now. We mainly talk about books. I like having a book club of two.

I have lasagne in the oven at the moment, waiting for her to arrive. On the worktop is our latest book club read. I pick it up again. I'd been enjoying it at first, but all of a sudden the loneliness of the story came seeping through the pages and into my soul. I surprised myself by feeling angry, even putting the book down at one point and not picking it up again for a while. But I want to have it read by tomorrow. I might start it again. I can skim read if necessary.

There's no time now as a knock comes on the door and I go to greet my friend. And as long as Eva keeps quiet, or I play a radio in the background, there's no way Milly will know there's anyone else in the house besides the two of us.

DAY 2

14 August 2019

CHAPTER SEVEN

Eva

Eva woke with a start. She sat up quicker than she should have and her vision became blurred for a few seconds. A rush of nausea came over her and she staggered across to the bucket, getting there just in time to throw up. There was a little urine in it from the day before, where she'd had to stoop over it to relieve herself. The stench of it made her retch again.

Afterwards, trying not to panic as dark thoughts of what her captor might do to her infiltrated her mind, she sat so still that she ached when she stretched out a limb. Since arriving there, wherever there was, she had struggled to shake off whatever drug she'd been given.

She knew she'd been administered something because of her lack of memory. She wondered if it was Rohypnol. She'd researched the drug last year as part of a feature she'd written about date rape, so she was aware of its many side effects. She had been feeling drowsy and dizzy, with a loss of motor control and co-ordination. Stomach disturbances was another one she recalled.

Her head pounded like a drum, and she was having trouble focusing in the dim light through her good eye. But she pushed herself.

Hoping to be clearer now, she tried once more to think of how she'd got here, why she had woken up in the room. The last thing she could recollect was being back at home, with Nick, in the kitchen. She recalled them spending time together the previous evening. He'd mentioned buying a card for his mum's birthday. She could see herself getting into her car and reversing out of the drive. After that, everything was blank.

Her eyes glistened with tears as she thought of her husband. She wondered if his team had put more pieces together, perhaps near to finding out where she was.

Even as she thought it, a sob escaped her. She didn't have to memorise her surroundings to recall at a later date. The room was exactly as the other three women had described it.

Who the hell was he to hold her captive? Why was he doing this?

Her left eye was really sore now. The swelling had worsened overnight. She tried not to touch it too much for fear of infecting it. Down here the dust was heavy, the room was filthy.

If it was the same captor as before, would she be set free after ten days? It was playing on her mind that the fourth woman hadn't come home. Poor Jill Bradshaw had gone missing but hadn't shown up on day ten, as everyone had hoped, following the pattern of the women before her. No one knew if she'd been taken by the same suspect, especially once the ten days had passed and there had been no sign of her. The national press had accused the police of doing nothing, almost as if they were waiting for the abductor to strike again, for him to make a mistake and lead them to him. Even now she realised how dangerous that was. She also knew it wasn't true. The police had been working tirelessly to solve the case, and to find Jill and bring her home.

Had he chosen Eva because she'd written the features on the abducted women? Had she been led to him because of it? Nick had warned her about getting too close. But she hadn't expected to be in danger because of it.

Or did the abductor want her to put his side to their readers? It happened a lot. Often Eva could put things right by sharing their story, but mud mostly stuck. It was a sad fact, but true.

Yesterday had already seemed like a week, and she thought about her team. What would they be thinking now? Would Charlie be feeling guilty for sending her out? It wasn't his fault, obviously. Eva was comforted that even though she couldn't recollect where she'd been going, at least the police could check her calendar.

It seemed ridiculous, and really it should be the furthest thing from her mind, but she was lost without her phone. The first thing she did when she woke up was check out the news channels. Next it was her email and social media channels. As a journalist, she used her own account to share news too. She was always scrolling, and retweeting things of interest. Being the first to break a story or make a comment about one that went a little viral was such a personal thrill.

Of course, there were the times when she'd been a victim of trolling. The warrior keyboard squad loved nothing more than spewing out their vitriol and getting others to jump on for maximum exposure. Most of the time it went over her head. Occasionally, she'd get some weirdo who became hell-bent on making her life hell for a few days. Other than that the occasional threat of rape, beating or death went recorded by the paper but was not acted upon, unless necessary.

The world had gone a little crazy since social media had become such a big player in many people's lives. When she'd first started working for the newspaper, a lot of things had been predominantly in print. Now the world had moved on to digital, and even though it had made things easier in some respects, in others it had become a nuisance. Still, she was one of the lucky ones to keep her job.

Eva hadn't worked for anyone else but the *Stoke News*, prided herself on that fact, yet she knew with everything it boiled down to politics and finances. She was always dreading the day they would go all digital and lose half, if not more, of their staff. She just prayed her job would be safe.

And yet, there were things that she didn't like about her role too. She hated invading people's grief and angst for a story. Sure she was sensitive but others were not.

She speculated about what people might be saying about her now.

Serves her right for sticking her nose in where it's not wanted.

She must have made things worse by writing about it.

Do you think this is a revenge abduction?

I wonder if he'll kill someone this time?

She closed her eyes and tried to think of happier things. But how could she? She needed to tell herself over and over that she was going to get out.

She wasn't going to let her captor get to her.

She was going home.

CHAPTER EIGHT

Alex

I come downstairs around half past seven and flick on the kettle. I've had a good night's rest considering my exertion the day before. There's something about the power that makes me sleep like a baby, content and almost heavy.

On the monitor, I can see Eva curled up on the mattress, the blanket tucked up under her chin. I'm not sure if she's asleep. She'll probably still be dozy while the drugs wear off. I'll make her some breakfast, to be kind today at least.

Eva had been so easy to capture. I only had to make one phone call and she was over at my house, offering to help. She's a very trusting soul, nice with it too. She really does care about people, silly cow. We chatted for a while and then I slipped the drug into a mug of tea. The rest was easy. Getting her down into the cellar, exchanging her clothes for the grey drab she's now wearing. Removing her jewellery and shoes. Then setting on her.

I look down at my hands. They're a little swollen after the beating I gave her. I'll need to be careful at work so that no one notices them. I snort. That won't be a problem, as hardly anyone observes me.

I know what you're thinking: how can I do what I do and then go out to work as if I don't have a woman held captive in my cellar?

Well, I can assure you it isn't easy being me. I have to find money from somewhere, for the essentials. Things to keep me alive. And blending into civilisation day after day suits me.

I take the tray down to the cellar. After I've unlocked the hatch, Eva slides the one from last night back to me and then I pass through the other one. There are two slices of toast and butter on a paper plate, and tea in a paper cup. There's no spoon, nothing that can be used as a weapon. I don't care if she takes sugar or has it black. She has two choices: to drink the tea or not drink at all.

'Do you have a painkiller, please?' Eva asks. 'I have a headache and I've been sick.'

I silently scoff. You'd think she'd be begging me to let her out, screaming until she was hoarse at the audacity of it all. Well, she can ask me for anything but she isn't going to get it. The purpose of me holding her against her will is for her to suffer. No one gave me painkillers when I was locked up and hurt.

I say nothing, leave her to her breakfast and set off for work. It's raining, so I pull my coat in closer, my collar turned up. I like the feeling of anonymity it gives me.

It's only a ten-minute walk to the stop. The bus arrives and I climb aboard, sitting down at the back.

I see the same people day after day. The woman in her fifties with the short blonde bob, always head down scrolling through her phone. She's smiled at me a few times, but when I haven't returned it, she hasn't bothered again. Now she avoids any empty seats next to me.

The man in his late teens who plays the music so loud I can hear the incessant tinny beat as he moves his head in time to the rhythm. He gets off two stops before me. I've often wanted to follow him, see if he walks down any dark alley or cut-through, so I could punch his lights out. It's just plain rude to be that annoying.

I spend a lot of time plotting to hurt people I don't know. It's the only thing that makes me happy on my commute into the city centre. Thinking of what I could do to others while I don't interact with anyone at all. That's how I like to be – on the periphery. I've got so used to it over the years that it comes easy to me now. People will bump into me as they rush around and I'll be the one to apologise.

In the office, I'll walk with my head down, avoiding all eye contact. I'm the computer geek, doing the menial jobs that make other people's lives easier. You know 'switch it off and on again'. No one notices me until a laptop crashes or the main server goes down.

I could have excelled at my job, done something different and scaled the heights to the top. But my plan is more important to me – the most significant thing in my life.

Still, none of this would have happened if she hadn't got in touch last year. I thought she'd want to see me, try to put things right. But I couldn't let her. We've been emailing though, gearing up to meet again. That is something to look forward to. She'll realise then I'm not that weakling she left behind. She will recognise that I'm stronger now. I may seem all mild, but it's an act, you see. To ensure my anonymity.

I knew she'd contact me but it's painful after all this time. She let me down so badly. And now because of her, here we are. The final jigsaw pieces are being slotted together. This is my time to shine, at last. Soon there will be no more staying in the background.

I will be in one of Eva's features this time.

MARCH 2019

CHAPTER NINE

Stoke News

Second Woman Missing
Eva Farmer, Senior News Reporter
15 March 2019

Staffordshire Police are looking into the disappearance of local woman, Maxine Stallington, 66. Mrs Stallington, who lives in Blurton, Stoke-on-Trent, was last seen on 12 March at 11 a.m. getting off a bus on her way to visit a friend for coffee.

Mrs Stallington is a widow and lives alone. The police were alerted by her eldest daughter, Sandra Jackson, when she failed to come home that evening and there was no contact from her phone. Sandra, 39, said it's as if her mother disappeared into thin air and is extremely worried about her after the abduction of another woman, two months ago.

Stephanie Harvey, 36, was abducted in the city in January but turned up ten days after she went missing. She has no recollection of where she was during that time and has been unable to help the police find out who kidnapped her.

'My mum went missing after arranging to meet a friend,' Sandra said. 'It isn't like her not to turn up and then not to answer her phone. She's not in the best of health at the moment, either. She suffers poor mobility on most days.'

Sandra, and her siblings, James and Kathryn, insist their mother wouldn't be doing this purposely.

'This is totally out of character,' James added. 'She calls us all daily, if not more often. She'd never be away from her phone. We're really worried about her.'

DCI Stan Hedley, Senior Investigating Officer, said, 'It's too early for assumptions that the two cases are connected and we need to keep an open mind at the moment. But we are listening to the family, as well as monitoring all channels and following up leads from the general public.

'We urge everyone to think back to what they were doing around the time she went missing, and to contact us if they can think of anything, no matter how trivial.'

CHAPTER TEN

Eva

Eva walked up the drive of a large semi-detached house on the outskirts of the city. The road was on the edge of a well-kept estate. A small hatchback sat in front of an integral garage. She knocked on the front door.

A woman in her mid-sixties answered it. She was of medium build, wearing her white-blonde hair tied back, faded jeans and an oversized jumper. Her face was sagging with age, or weight loss, it was hard to tell. But she had a welcoming smile below bright blue eyes.

'Hello, Mrs Stallington.' Eva held up her ID card. 'Thank you for agreeing to see me.'

She was shown into the living room. It was decorated in an aubergine and tangerine palette, quite pleasing to the eye. The retro look suited the woman who had let her in, showing a fun side to her. Eva wondered if it was a true representation of her now.

'I've been following your reports,' Maxine told her, standing in front of the fireplace.

'So you will know I don't sensationalise anything.' Eva placed a hand on her arm. 'I'm so sorry that you've had to go through this.' Eva got out her notepad and sat down. 'Do you mind if I take some notes?'

Eva watched as Maxine visibly relaxed. She had her trust and she wouldn't abuse it.

'How have you been since your return?' she asked first.

'I feel like I'm in a catch-22 situation: I'm so relieved to be free but equally upset that I was taken.'

As Maxine shuddered, Eva wondered if she was back in the room again. Memories flashing at her.

'I wondered if I would get home. I kept thinking that perhaps Stephanie Harvey wasn't supposed to have come out of the situation alive. That's what was going through my head. I wasn't sure if I would survive for ten days either.'

'You were kept in a cellar that you think was the same one as Stephanie Harvey?'

'Yes, it was about a three-metre square. There was a mattress to sleep on with one sheet, and a bucket in the corner of the room. It was emptied during the night. That's how I knew I'd been given something to make me sleep, most probably in liquid form.'

'I bet it was hard to be alone for so long.'

'I lay there often, thinking of how to take my own life.'

The tears welling in Maxine's eyes matched Eva's. How low must the woman have been to think of suicide?

'But there was no way to do it. How could I, stuck in a room on my own? There was nothing to tie a bed sheet to. There was nothing to cut myself with. It was useless.' Maxine grimaced. 'I thought about my children a lot. My son, James, and his wife had a child on the way. I wondered if I'd ever see him born. Luckily I did. We now have Rudy.' She pointed to a photo on the mantelpiece of a man with a small baby. 'He's six days old and keeps me going, I can tell you.'

Eva smiled, that longing for a child of her own burning deep inside. Rudy was all thick dark hair and dimples.

'And he never said a word to you?' she questioned.

'No. I can't recall anything about my release either. And I have tried and tried and tried.' Maxine banged the palm of her hand on her thigh in time with her words, her face creasing in anger. 'That bloody tattoo on my neck is a constant reminder of what happened to me too.'

Eva watched in voyeuristic horror as Maxine moved aside her hair and showed it to her.

'I'm going to have it covered up. It's visible, so I might as well look at something I like, something personal to me, rather than a memory of… that time. I thought of a rose. My husband, Barry, was the love of my life. I'd prefer to think about him when I look at it.'

'And you have no idea who would do this to you?' Eva hoped her questions weren't coming across as accusatory to Maxine. That wasn't her intention.

But Maxine didn't seem offended as she shook her head. 'The police kept asking me questions. Did I see who it was? Did I know where I was held? But I couldn't tell them anything. All I can say is that my recollection is the same as Stephanie's. How could anyone hold someone against their will for so long for no apparent reason?'

Eva left a few minutes later. She drove away and then pulled up in the next street for a breather. What Maxine had been through was harrowing and it was rubbing off on her. She swallowed a sob as she wiped away tears.

How could anyone do that to a person? Lock them up, not talk to them, no interaction. It was cruel, beyond words.

And totally beyond her comprehension.

DAY 2

14 August 2019

CHAPTER ELEVEN

Eva

Eva had been feeling sick all morning, but now she'd been alone with her thoughts for hours, she found herself starving. She hoped it was her system getting back to normal after the vomiting.

The light coming in through the tiny window was bright. There were no shadows in the room yet, although she was dreading them when they came later in the day. She stood up and paced the room, counting seven steps to one wall and eight steps to the other. It kept her body active, but her mind wouldn't switch off.

There was so much she could think about but didn't want to. She tried to conjure up happy thoughts. Nick's face sprang to her mind but that made her cry. He was her protector, her lover, her friend all in one. The last thing she could recall was the film they'd watched together. A cheesy horror fest full of zombies and blood that they'd both enjoyed.

She thought of her work colleagues rallying round to get word out about her abduction. That made her cry too.

She thought of her family and friends, and Jill, the last missing woman who hadn't come home.

Hunger made her stomach cramp. If all she was to get was a bit of toast in the morning and a sandwich for her supper, she'd better get used to the pangs that were going to ravage her. All three women she'd interviewed had spoken of going hungry, having to beg for food and water. She didn't want to plead for anything, but she would if she had to. It was inhumane how she was being kept. The least he could do was to treat her with a little respect.

She laughed out loud, making herself jump in the still of the room. Who was she trying to kid? He couldn't have a conscience. All he had was a plan; one that she now featured in.

Was it only yesterday that she couldn't recollect? She would have been missed from around lunchtime. Her phone would be full of messages and emails. Then the police would be notified.

She squeezed her eyes to stop the tears from falling as she imagined the look of horror on Nick's face as he was told, of his utter devastation. But she would have a good team looking for her. She laughed inwardly: she would know most of them.

Eva would have been online news and over the waves some time yesterday afternoon, perhaps earlier. Her work colleagues would be worried, her friends too, and she assumed they would have been contacted to see if she had turned up unannounced. And once everyone had been checked and she was nowhere to be seen, then people would assume she was a victim of the kidnapper.

They would be looking for her. They'd be here soon, she repeated to herself over and over.

She had been consumed since January with the thought of who he could be, why he was abducting women and holding them against their will. One thing she was thankful for: so far, he hadn't sexually assaulted any of them. She couldn't imagine having to go through that as well as being trapped there. There'd been a lot of talk about him being impotent and this was his way of gaining control. She shook her head to rid herself of the thoughts.

'Five, four, three, two, one. Everything is fine,' she said to calm herself again. It didn't work and she burst into tears, sitting down on the edge of the mattress. If only there was some way she could get out.

In frustration, she rushed to the door, lay down in front of it and kicked at the wood that was on the other side of the pet flap. She knew she couldn't climb through it even if she could kick off the hatch. And her feet were bare; she'd break something before the wood gave way. Still, she tried, until her feet were too sore and her tears came again.

She sat against the door. Could she really get through this? This torture, this silence. It was going to be some test of her mental strength.

CHAPTER TWELVE

Alex

It's been agony sitting in the office today. There is so much going on and I have to work hard to get to everyone who has issues. It's mostly down to too much traffic to the main server. I'm not a miracle worker but I do the best I can. Not sure why I bother so much though, when everyone is so ungrateful.

All I want to do is go home and be with Eva, watch her on the monitor. I did think of booking some time off, but I want to save a few days for next week, when things will be more interesting. Plus I need everything to seem as normal as possible.

I finally get through the day, and it's when I'm on the bus again, I can sit back to relax and read the *Stoke News*. Eva is everywhere on the first five pages. It makes interesting reading as I travel home.

She seems to be liked by a lot of people, but then again, isn't that always the case when something like this happens? It's all about sympathy for them, when I'm the real victim here.

There's another photo of Eva with Nick. A picture-perfect couple. Not like my mum and Ian, but like my mum and dad. I was robbed when my dad died: we all were. If only he'd survived, none of this would be happening right now.

I wonder if Eva has worked out yet how she came to be in my cellar. Does she think she's been on a night out with friends? Is she questioning if her drink was spiked?

I stop at the local shop once I'm off the bus. I'm treating myself tonight, as I might not be able to buy some of my favourite food when I leave the country next week. I've bought millionaire shortbread cheesecake and a bottle of red, although I'm trying to keep my head straight until this is over.

I let myself into the house, the low rumble of the radio greeting me as I walk through to the kitchen. The monitor shows Eva sitting on the mattress, her back against the wall. She's hugging her knees again. Poor thing, I laugh. She seems extremely lonely, vulnerable too. Good! She deserves to feel that way.

A memory comes back to me in Technicolor and I have to sit down for a moment. I was in a room with my back against the wall. I too was hugging my knees. But I was ten years old. My brother wasn't with me and I was crying for him. He'd been naughty, or so Ian had thought. Ian was the man my mother shacked up with when our wonderful father died.

But it wasn't Jude who had been naughty. It was me, and Jude had taken the blame. We were messing around and I had spilt my juice over the carpet. It had made a terrible stain and we both knew I'd be in trouble for it. It wouldn't be seen as an accident. I would be punished.

And then I could hear him in the other room, crying because Ian was shouting at him. Hitting him.

I see myself covering my ears, trying to block out the noise. How cruel could one man be? There was so much I shouldn't have gone through as a child. And it was all their fault.

I shake off the melancholy. I mustn't let things like that get to me. It's in my past now and, once Eva has done her ten days, I can move on and not have to think of it again.

Childhood is supposed to be the best part of your life but, mark my words, it isn't unless you have loving parents. And even then, it can change in a heartbeat. The world you know and love can disappear totally in a few weeks. A death, a funeral. A new man. I pinch the bridge of my nose to block out any more images. Believe me, there are a lot of them.

I reach for the bottle of whisky, pour two fingers and drink it back neat. I need to steady my nerves. Nothing is going to take me back to that time. Nothing at all. I will never give them the satisfaction of it hurting me. I was ten years old, I was a child, and I didn't deserve what happened to me. Neither did Jude.

I look at Eva on the monitor again. She still hasn't moved. Perhaps she is sleeping. Time to go and see her, I think. That will make me feel much better.

CHAPTER THIRTEEN

Eva

Eva wasn't sure how long she'd been sitting staring at the wall in front of her. There was no sense of time. She could have been here hours or overnight and she wouldn't know. There was no way she could tell.

Then she froze. There was a rumble of sound, as if there was a muted conversation going on. Was there a radio on? Or could there be someone else here with her captor? She prayed they wouldn't hurt her again.

Another noise. It sounded like a door opening. She listened. Her heartbeat ratcheted up so loudly that she was sure he would hear it. She gasped as footsteps stopped outside the door.

'Hello?' she whispered, her voice cracking it was so hoarse. 'Help! Can you hear me?'

The hatch opened and she got to her knees, looking through. But all she could see were steps in front of her, against another wall.

'Hello? Who's out there? Please. Let me out. I'm trapped. Being held against my will.' She stopped and listened. 'Will someone help me?' she screamed.

She waited but there was no noise, no movement, no sound. But as she turned to go back to the mattress, she heard something.

Coming through the hole was a newspaper, which dropped to the floor. Eva reached for it. There was a note written on the front of it.

YOU HAVE 30 MINS TO READ AND THEN I WANT IT BACK BEFORE YOU CAN HAVE ANY FOOD.

The front page was all about her. She shuffled back to the mattress and read the words greedily:

Stoke News

Journalist Missing for Two Days
14 August 2019

Police are concerned and looking into the disappearance of journalist Eva Farmer. Eva, 33, works here at Stoke News. She lives in Stockton Brook with her husband, Detective Constable Nick Farmer.

Eva had recently written an article regarding the four women who have been abducted over the past six months and it is feared she may have become the latest victim.

The police were alerted when Eva failed to come into the office at lunchtime and was unreachable by phone. Eva's last entry in her work's calendar showed a meeting, but she never arrived for it. Her vehicle was found this morning in a nearby car park.

'Eva is meticulous when it comes to personal safety,' editor-in-chief, Charlie Peterson, said. 'She and the whole team are – it's something we drill into anyone who works for us. It's a sad fact that as journalists we get our fair share of threats, so we make equally sure that our whereabouts are noted down.

'Eva texted her PA first thing on the morning she went missing to say who she was meeting. I'm very worried about her, especially after the recent kidnappings. It doesn't bear thinking about.'

Husband Nick, 35, a serving police officer, says it is unlike Eva to go this long without contact. 'She is always meticulous in letting someone know her whereabouts due to the nature of her job. I'm extremely concerned for her safety, and I just want her home.'

DCI Stan Hedley, Senior Investigating Officer, said that a man in his forties, alleged to have had a meeting arranged with Eva, was helping them with their enquiries. The police are also reaching out to the general public to try and jog memories. 'Eva hasn't used her phone, nor been in contact with her family or friends,' he commented. 'We urge everyone to think about what they were doing around the time she went missing, and to contact us if they can recall anything and get in touch with us on the helpline printed below.'

Eva gasped. Who was the man they spoke of? She was meeting someone? She tried to recall it but nothing would come.

Could it be him, her abductor? Could he have lured her here somehow? But if he was the same person, surely he would be in police custody right now?

It can't be him. They were talking to the wrong man.

Tears dripped down her face and onto the newspaper as she stared at the image of Nick. The photo was one of them together. They had been at a wedding last summer, raising a glass to each other as the photo was taken. Eva remembered how happy they'd been that day. Nick had become besotted by a guest's four-month-old son, and they'd chatted about starting a family of their own. They'd both decided the timing was right to start planning for their own child shortly afterwards.

She willed Nick and his team to find out where she was and come and get her. She needed him now, more than ever. He wouldn't let her down. He would get her out of here.

She had to hold on to that thought.

FEBRUARY 2019

CHAPTER FOURTEEN

Alex and Milly

It's school half-term and I have booked the day off. Milly is due soon. She's coming for lunch and I'm looking forward to it. The kitchen is pretty dismal, not somewhere a teenager would want to hang out, but I always have lots of food to eat and it's warm. Not like Winterdale Children's Home.

Milly doesn't like school: I loved and hated it in equal measure. Every class has a quiet one, a brainy one who loves learning. Milly told me one of the girls, Jaimie, calls her a swot. She says sometimes she does worse in her tests so that she won't be singled out. I think back to our conversation last week.

'I hate my life,' Milly had said quietly.

I don't think she'd expected me to hear her.

When she didn't say anything else, I urged her to continue. 'Come on, spit it out. What's bothering you?'

And just like that, Milly was telling me everything.

'I'm fifteen years old and I have no friends,' she finished. 'There are three girls, one named Jaimie, who makes my life hell every day.'

'Why do they do that?'

'I don't know. It started when I moved up to high school. They were from a different school and they started to pick on me straight away. The girls are in a group who everyone loves.' She scoffed. 'Well, at least it seems that way. Either that or they're scared of being themselves. They really are so mean.'

'What do they do?' Anger burned inside me at Milly's reaction. I could see tears in her eyes. It wasn't easy for her to tell me, but I encouraged her to continue.

Milly shrugged. 'They push me into furniture or doors as they barge past. They knock my bag from my shoulder so that everyone thinks I'm clumsy. They rip pages from my exercise books.'

'And what do your teachers say?'

'I don't tell them.' She examined her fingernails rather than look at me. 'The worst thing is when most of the class joins in and laughs at me too. I try to ignore it but sometimes I can't.'

I clenched my fists, barely able to contain my anger.

'I don't even have a best friend.' She wiped at a tear that had escaped and glanced at me. 'Except you, of course.'

I smiled at her. Although we are an odd combination, it seemed as if she felt better once she'd let it all out. She knew she could trust me, and I like that.

'I don't know what to do about Jaimie,' she had added. 'I've tried being nice, keeping away from her, but nothing works. She and her friends follow me everywhere, trying to cause trouble.'

'Sheep.' I nodded, knowingly. 'You'll always find a leader who others will follow. They fear the same retaliation if they don't join in, whether they like what's happening or not. They don't want to be the butt of anyone's jokes, so they laugh at other people's expense. There are a lot of people like that. I hate bullies. Someone should teach that Jaimie a lesson so she doesn't do anything like this again.'

'It would make my life easier.'

'Bullies always get their comeuppance.' I took a deep breath and let it out with a huge sigh of frustration. 'I was the quiet kid in school, the one who no one wanted to know. I was so lonely. But at least you have me to talk to every now and then.'

Milly smiled through watery eyes.

'You're going to be okay,' I told her, and she nodded.

'I have to go.' She sighed. 'And we haven't even discussed this week's book.'

'Good, because I haven't finished it, if I'm honest.'

Milly grinned. 'Can we talk about it next week?'

I had glanced around the living room once I'd said goodbye to Milly. I was sure if anyone found out about her coming to see me they'd put a stop to it. That's why she'll always be my secret friend. Even now, I can't stop thinking about what she said about Jaimie. I'm going to do something about that for her. Milly needs my help. But before I can plan any more, there's a knock on the door and I get to my feet. Milly is here. I rush to let her in.

'Hello, Mils. Come on in. I've made a cake. You can help me to devour it.'

'Sounds good to me!' She steps in with a smile.

As she follows me through to the kitchen, I feel myself relax. At least I can dive into the world of Stephen King as we discuss our latest book club read.

DAY 3

15 August 2019

CHAPTER FIFTEEN

Eva

Eva woke herself up crying out in her sleep. Upset to see she was alone, she let the tears continue. She'd been dreaming about Nick. They were on holiday, somewhere warm with a beach. They'd rushed into the sea, messing about, splashing water over each other, and suddenly they'd begun to swim out to sea. Nick was further and further away from her and she couldn't keep up. When she looked around she couldn't see him, nor could she reach the beach. She was treading water, then going underneath it. Screaming each time she could take a breath, getting nowhere. She couldn't help herself. She was going to drown.

But she'd woken up in a panic, just as she went under the water once more.

She was certain now that her captor was slipping something in her food to make her sleep, but she didn't care. She longed to drop off quickly, to be taken away from her anxiety. The days went so slowly. The silence during the long daylight hours was as much as she could cope with: it gave her too much time to think.

She sat up, the feeling of nausea assaulting her again, and she raced across to the bucket in the corner of the room. Her hair was lank after being unwashed for so long. Its texture was greasy as she pushed it behind her ears, holding it to the side of her face as she vomited again.

It was then her body went cold. She looked back into the bucket at the liquid she'd thrown up. There wasn't much in it due to her lack of food. Yet there should have been diarrhoea mixed with urine. But the vomit was all there was.

Someone had been in and emptied the bucket. While she was sleeping.

The thought made her retch again, fear overtaking her, and she gasped for air. She hadn't heard anyone come into the room and that scared her.

She managed to crawl back to the bed, wrapping the thin sheet around herself despite the warmth. The day was just beginning and yet she couldn't bear to think of spending another hour in there. The nights were surely helped with a sedative: Eva presumed it was mashed into the cheese spread, so fine she couldn't see or taste it, or added to her tea. Still, the benefit of being completely knocked out outweighed everything at the moment.

Above her, she could hear noises. A chair being dragged from underneath a table. A TV or radio playing low. A door closing. Every now and then, the pipes would bang. The sounds of life reminding her that she was trapped down here.

After interviewing the other three victims, Eva feared the worst. The reason that Jill Bradshaw hadn't come home wasn't lost on her. Was she here, locked in another room she didn't know about? Had the maniac murdered her? Would he kill Eva too? She tried to shut down her thoughts.

Breakfast was delivered to her but Eva didn't say a word this time. She was afraid of trying to communicate and being met with silence.

After she'd eaten – two slices of toast and a cup of tea: the same as yesterday – she decided to lie down again. But she couldn't settle.

She didn't want to show him how upset she was either, yet she wanted to cry. So she pulled the sheet over her head and sobbed.

She could almost feel Nick beside her. She physically ached, wanting to put her arms around him. For him to turn over, reach for her and kiss her until they melted into one. Talk to her, ask what's for tea, chat about trivial things.

The thought that she might not ever see anyone, or be part of anything again was too much to bear. She'd hoped crying might release some tension, but it hadn't worked. Her heart yearned for the past, and yet she didn't want to think of the future.

And it was still barely the start of a new day.

CHAPTER SIXTEEN

Alex

It's quite exciting getting on the bus knowing what's going on at my house and yet also aware that no one knows what I'm doing. No one will look at me and think that I'm the one in the newspapers. That I have kidnapped five women.

I walk down the aisle as the bus drives off, making my way to the back, to one of three spare seats. The boy with the headphones is two seats in front and I can hear the racket, see his head nodding like one of those stupid dogs in rear car windows that had been all the rage when I was ten. The woman next to him doesn't seem to be bothered though, as she expertly applies her make-up while the bus trundles along.

I wonder what they'd think if they knew what I'd done. How I had hurt so many women; how I've held their futures in my hands.

Although I wish I could keep Eva longer. She's nice. I like her. Maybe I can have some fun with her. Of course, it would be cruel but I don't care. The worse the better, as far as I'm concerned.

I stare out of the window, watching everyone rushing around to get to their next destination. School and work mostly, I guess. As the bus slows for traffic lights, I think of Eva again, alone in my cellar. She is hidden away, at my mercy. I like that.

I snigger, and the woman across from me gives me a funny look. I roll my eyes. Jeez, you can't even laugh nowadays without someone being offended.

I'm particularly pleased with how Eva is behaving, though. She seems to be settling in quite well. I had thought she might make more noise. Perhaps it's because of the article she wrote. In some ways, she's known more of what to expect than anyone, after the women I set free told her everything.

Stephanie Harvey did nothing but cry. She practically screamed the house down at one point. I ended up leaving the radio on quite high during the day in case anyone heard her. She soon calmed down after I drugged her again and gave her a good beating. Funny, when she came round the next morning, she was as quiet as a mouse.

I wonder what Eva can hear from the cellar. Does she know she's all alone, that I've gone out? Perhaps she hears the front door closing. I know she can hear me pottering around in the kitchen because she's right underneath me. It's not a problem. I'm just curious to know.

Still, she'll break at some point, just like the others did, I'm sure of it. And I'll be waiting when that happens.

The bus stops and several people get on. The woman doing her make-up pops everything in her bag again, checking herself one last time in the mirror with a pout. I think she works in one of the larger shops on Stafford Street. Every day, she gets off at the next stop and I see her turn the corner before the bus moves on again.

I wonder what she does with herself all day. Maybe she has a lot of friends, has lunch with them, then goes home to her husband. Perhaps a family.

And then I see them and I'm instantly transferred to a place I don't want to be reminded of. A woman bustles on with a child. The boy is the same age as Jude was when he died. He slides along a seat and she sits next to him. I see them laughing at something the woman is sharing with him on her phone. The boy's laughter is infectious, but it makes my blood boil. How can Jude have died in such a cruel way?

I miss him so much. I miss my mum too, when she was like that. She had been, before she met Ian. Jude and I were so happy then. When Dad was alive and we were a proper family.

I don't think I'll ever want a family. I know the pain of not getting things right, how a child suffers if it's not wanted. A child gives you unconditional love, but I can never love anyone in return. I am damaged goods. I have no emotions. I am soulless. A shadow of how I should be.

And it's all her fault.

At my stop, I almost burst from the bus in a bubble of breathlessness. I stand for a moment at the side of a wall until it passes. I can't bear to be reminded of Jude. Because it brings back the memories of everything else.

MAY 2019

CHAPTER SEVENTEEN

Stoke News

Third woman missing in five months
Eva Farmer, Senior News Reporter
16 May 2019

Staffordshire Police are concerned over the disappearance of Alison Green, 39, from Dresden. The police were alerted by her husband when Alison failed to return from the supermarket after a quick phone call to say she was on her way home. She was last seen getting off a bus yesterday morning a few minutes from where she lives.

Husband Steve, 41, said, 'Alison messaged me to ask if there was anything I needed. That was the last I heard from her. She never arrived home. I don't know what to think, except for the possibility that if someone is holding her, she will be set free in ten days. Our daughters are worried too. We're all trying not to fear the worst.'

DCI Stan Hedley, Senior Investigating Officer, said, 'We're looking into this abduction, in particular the similarities between the recent abductions of two women from within the Stoke areas.

'Stephanie Harvey, 36, was abducted in January but turned up ten days after she went missing. Sixty-six-year-old Maxine

Stallington was abducted on 12 March and was also released after ten days.

'It's extremely worrying and we are working with all three families, as well as monitoring channels and following up leads from the general public.'

CHAPTER EIGHTEEN

Eva

Eva lay in bed that night thinking of the interview she'd done earlier that day. She'd spoken to Alison Green's family. It had been a tough job for her this time. Meeting with Stephanie Harvey, Maxine Stallington and their families had been hard, but knowing what those two women had been through now meant that Alison's relatives were understandably more upset. They kept surmising the details, praying that she would be home soon.

It was the hope the Green family were clinging on to that made Eva so angry with the situation after visiting them. The eternal faith that everything would be okay come day ten, even if Alison came back as a different person to when they'd last seen her.

It was hard to imagine Alison could be locked up in the same room that the first two women had described in almost identical details. Twice over the past few months, Eva had awoken from nightmares after imagining she'd been kidnapped too. The second time she'd woken up crying, Nick had consoled her, hugging her tightly until her heart rate was back to normal.

It wasn't often she took her work home with her. Mostly, she covered easier cases; if there were bad ones, she tended to compartmentalise. But this one had got under her skin. And yet still there were no motives.

A tentative link was possibly coming through. All three women were or had worked in the support sector. If Alison did come back, it was looking likely that may be a connection.

Nick had been keeping her updated with what he could share about the police leads. Stephanie Harvey and Maxine Stallington didn't know each other personally, nor professionally, in any capacity. At the moment, the police were going through their records, the cases they had worked on, to see if there was a connection there, and this would take a while.

Nick and his team had already gone back to the time when the two women had been working in the services. They were now overlapping the details of Alison Green, but without her to speak to it would obviously be harder.

Even though the police were working relentlessly behind the scenes, there had been no positive leads from the public, and nothing from the CCTV cameras. The kidnapper was treading carefully, only going to places where invisibility would be possible.

Beside her, Nick's eyes were closed but she knew he wasn't asleep yet.

'Do you still think it's a coincidence?' she asked, idly stroking his chest. 'Two women with no connections are abducted and returned, and now a third missing?'

'It's looking unlikely.' He sighed. 'If we don't find her before, I suppose after ten days we'll know for sure. If our perp lets her go at the same time.'

'It could be part of a bigger plan. Maybe she'll be held longer. She might not even be released at all. I mean, who knows why the other two women were set free?'

'It seems a hideous game to play, not just on the victims but on their families too.'

'She might have been drugged the whole time she was there and not recall anything.'

'Yes, we're aware of that.'

'How is anyone to know if she can't remember?'

'Oi, I'll have you know we're covering all those angles.' He looked at her before rolling his eyes.

'I know, I know. It's just so sad, isn't it? Awful for their loved ones.'

'I'd be lost without you if you disappeared for ten days.'

'Yeah, right.' Eva giggled. 'You'd probably be glad of the time on your own!'

'Don't joke about it.'

'Sorry. I guess it could happen to anyone if you don't have any idea where the victims are being held.'

'Which is why I keep telling you not to step over the line with your features.'

'Since when have I ever done that?' She slapped his arm playfully.

'You know what I mean.'

Nick turned out the light and they settled down for the night. Still sleep wouldn't come to Eva, things running round her head. She would have to wait until the ten days were up to hear the fate of Alison Green, like everyone else.

DAY 3

15 August 2019

CHAPTER NINETEEN

Alex

I retrieve the newspaper from my bag and take it down to the cellar with me. I write the same note on the top and push it through the hatch. Then I go back upstairs while I give Eva half an hour to read it.

The *Stoke News* is still running Eva's story over the first few pages. I wonder if they would cover it for so long if it was anyone else. It seems a perk of the job to hog the limelight like that.

Yet, over the months, with each woman I've abducted, the media attention has been more and more. When I took Stephanie Harvey, I bet people didn't know what to make of it. For all everyone knew, she could have gone off with another man. She could have killed herself and they were waiting to find a body. She could have had an accident and been left with amnesia, unable to tell anyone who she was.

Then imagine how people reacted when Maxine Stallington went missing too. I bet they were all dying to know who I was by then. The press went mad; the coverage was addictive. I read every article written about me. Eva was still the most generous journalist by far, with her ability to see things from both sides.

After Alison Green, and then Jillian Bradshaw, I had everyone's attention. But I don't want to talk about Jillian. The memories are too painful.

Back to me. The feeling of power I get is electric. There's nothing like being the centre of attention by hiding the darkest secret. Everyone wants to know who I am, where I am and why I'm doing this. I'm glad it will all become clear by the end of next week.

I begin to prepare Eva's sandwich as I watch her scouring the paper. I pause when I see her linger at the page with the photo of her husband. A police officer, serving to protect. I snort. Well, he failed miserably on that count.

Eva's food is ready – the same cheese sandwich that she had the day before, plus a cup of tea – and I go back down to the cellar. When I open the hatch, the newspaper is pushed through it. I kick it out of the way and then put the tray on the floor. I shove it through and then turn to leave.

'Wait!' Eva cries behind me. 'Please don't go yet. Talk to me. I need to know why I'm here. Please!'

I leave her wondering if I've heard her. She isn't getting anything from me. What does she think she's in that room for? A bit of R&R? She is going to suffer, like I had to.

And I am happy to let her.

I hear the hourly news coming on the TV and sit to watch it while I eat my evening meal. It's shepherd's pie for me. I enjoy cooking and should have trained to be a chef if I'd thought more about it. If I wasn't so mixed up when it came to education.

It was very lonely going to school without Jude. I recall Maxine Stallington trying to coax me into some extra classes after school, but I didn't want to spend a moment longer in her company. Everyone pitied me. The only twin. I wanted to forget that as much as possible, and yet that meant trying to shut Jude out of my life too. It was so unfair.

Eva has a small slot on the local news and a mention on the national news. I smile with pride, relishing how I have everyone's attention. I bet people are talking about me everywhere. I wonder if the general public are actively looking out for me. I like this. It makes me happy.

But then as I switch to YouTube, a video I hate comes into view. The music takes me back to a time I don't wish to recollect: playing football in the garden with my mum and Jude, the three of us having fun while the radio was on. I cover my ears because I know what's coming next. Ian barrelling out and shouting at us all. We weren't allowed to have fun, especially when he was out.

It's so hard to stay in the zone all the time. The slightest memory can take me off balance. Sometimes I don't get straight again for weeks. I can't afford to go off the rails right now, so I switch the channel off altogether. It's better to watch something I've recorded. Something I know will make me laugh.

While I surf the channels in silence, I can't hear a peep from Eva. She is getting much better at staying quiet down there. I'm pleased really. I can't be doing with a noisy bitch, and I hate having to shut them up. Even if I don't care about Eva, I care about my own sanity. It's best that I stay as calm as I can over the next week or so. For everyone's sake.

I settle on a film to take my mind off things. It's an action movie, the first of the original Bourne trilogy. It will while away the evening too. Roll on tomorrow. One day closer to freedom. To everything being over. To revenge being emitted. To my sanity returning.

I close my eyes, thinking of sitting on a hot beach with a beer by my side. I've only booked a flight so far, to Ibiza. I think I'll get a hotel when I'm there. It's a much safer bet to not leave too many trails. It will be good to get a little sun on my back, join the throngs of summer holidaymakers. Of course, it will be quieter once the kids are at school next month but I'll be fine until then. At least I'll be out of here on the 22nd of August.

You see, I don't care about living in England any more. I can't see the point. I might as well go somewhere I can start again completely. I'm what's known as an emotional brick, yet I'm bored on my own. But I don't know if I can share intimacy with a partner again.

Not after what happened last time.

CHAPTER TWENTY

Eva

Eva curled up under the sheet, pulling it around her like a cocoon. The room was stickily hot but, even so, it felt like her shelter. Her protection against him while she waited for the sedatives to work. Even if she couldn't tell the time, she could see light outside the small window.

The effects of the drugs wore off too quickly, and she was often awake during the early hours. And she didn't feel anything like she had on that first morning, when she'd lost hours of her life from the day before. Back then she'd been exhausted, foggy-brained, a bit unsteady on her feet. She'd experienced that for most of the next day. Now, it took her a while to be fully awake but that was all. It was different, except for the vomiting. She didn't like that at all.

Eva thought back to reading the newspaper earlier. It had shaken her to see nothing new about her plight. Reading that the man who she was supposed to have met on the day she went missing wasn't being questioned any more had really upset her.

The police were still going through everything, with the hope of finding a link to all five women. Maybe they were keeping something to themselves, perhaps closer than they wanted the public to think. Because how could they link anyone to her except via her job? Not even she knew yet why she was being held.

The photo of her and Nick had made her cry again. The physical ache had intensified each time she saw him. She wished his image wasn't in the newspaper but, equally, she wanted it to be. She had to see what was happening on a day-to-day basis for as long as she could. And she knew that the police wouldn't be putting everything in the press. She hoped they were working on a substantial lead in the background to get her out of there. She had to keep that faith.

Would she ever see Nick again? She hoped so. She had to hang on to that optimism too.

There was hardly any noise from up above now, and she wondered if she was alone in the house again or not. Sounds were quickly becoming familiar to her. Occasionally she'd hear a bang that sounded like a car door. An engine faint in the background. And then nothing for hours as, she suspected, people went about their days outside their homes.

Her stomach rumbled. Bizarrely, her mouth salivated at the thought of the cakes she'd brought into work last week. It hadn't been anyone's birthday. She'd just wanted to treat her team, plus the lure of a chocolate cupcake with lime green icing had tempted her into the shop, its marketing job done as she'd come away with a box of six.

When she had hours by herself, it was everyday things like this she missed. Stupid simple things that she'd taken for granted, treats she'd dismissed as part of the job when, in actual fact, it was just that: a treat to be enjoyed, savoured. She swallowed, trying to imagine a taste of that cupcake right now, the icing melting on her tongue.

It made her feel better for all of ten seconds.

But it was another ten seconds she'd got herself through. And that was the main point of the exercise. Something to take her mind off this awful situation that she was in. To continue the countdown in her mind of days to freedom, and ignore the constant worry that she wouldn't be released on day ten, like Jillian Bradshaw. It was like car-crash TV: waiting for something to occur, but wanting to close her eyes to what it might be.

Besides, there was nothing else to think about. All day. Apart from what would happen to her on day ten.

CHAPTER TWENTY-ONE

Alex

I glance at the clock: 22:25.

I make my way into the kitchen and check everything is good on the monitor. Then I reach for my knife and open the door that leads me to the cellar. I switch on the light: wouldn't do to fall down the stairs. I try not to make a noise. I don't want to alert Eva as I press my ear to the door and listen. I can't hear anything.

As quietly as I can, I undo the lock on the hatch and open it wide, kneel down and peek inside. Eva is lying on the bed. There is light coming in from the main steps and I can see her face. Her eyes are closed.

I stand up and on the main door remove the padlock, pull away the chain and draw back the bolt. Then I pick up the knife again and step inside.

Eva is still lying on the bed, covers wrapped around her. Even though I know she'll be in a deep sleep, I step tentatively around her. Like I've done most evenings, I stand watching her breathing for a while, the rhythmic in and out of her gentle snore a welcome sound.

She's a beautiful woman. I can't see her eyes now but I remember them being sapphire blue and deep-set. Her hair is dark, layered to her shoulders with a sweeping fringe. Through her shape I can see she keeps herself fit and healthy. The arm out of the sheet is muscular and shapely, as if she lifts weights. Her nails are manicured; pity I'm going to spoil them.

I drop down in front of the mattress and gaze at her again. She has the look of an angel as she sleeps.

'You are a lucky woman, Eva,' I say quietly. 'When I let you go, everyone will want to know your story. This could be the making of you. I hear journalists talking about the one piece that made their career. Well, I'm handing this to you on a plate. You'll probably be asked to write a book. Perhaps they'll make a TV programme about your time here. Shame I won't be around to star in it.

'I'm sorry how things have turned out for you.' I stroke Eva's hair gently with a feather-light touch. 'But people need to know what me and Jude went through as kids. It's hard enough for me to talk about, let alone for others to read and believe, but I have to tell you.

'I was a child when that bastard killed my brother. I was convinced my mum would get away with it because, technically, she didn't cause it. She just went along with whatever he said. Even though I didn't like my foster home, I was glad she went to prison. She says she was a casualty, but don't you believe that, Eva. I was the innocent victim in all this.' I prod myself in the chest. 'And look at what it's made me do.'

Eva moves in her sleep, but her eyes remain closed. I smile, reassured there's no way she will wake up yet. Not after the dose of sedatives I mix with her food or drink every evening.

Finally, after a few minutes sitting with her, I pick up the bucket in the corner of the room, noticing she's been sick again. It's disgusting but par for the course. I replace it with the clean bucket I've brought down with me, leave the room and lock the door behind me.

'Sleep tight, Eva,' I say, before heading back upstairs.

APRIL 2019

CHAPTER TWENTY-TWO

Alex and Milly

'I'm so pleased you came.' I smile at Milly as she arrives at my house. 'How has your day been?'

She smiles back shyly. 'I got an A-star for my English essay!'

Milly sits down at the table while I bustle round preparing drinks.

'That's fantastic news,' I reply. 'Did you write about that idea I mentioned to you?'

'Yeah, you're a genius. Everyone was intrigued about my café book club. Mrs Matthews, that's my English teacher, said I had a vivid imagination and that she loved the characters in it.'

'That's brilliant. And how's school been lately?'

'So-so.' Milly smiles, but it doesn't reach her eyes.

'What's wrong? You seem so sad.'

'Oh, it's nothing.'

'Is it Jaimie and her crew again?'

'Can we change the subject? I don't want to talk about her.' Milly pauses. 'What about you?'

'Me?'

'Yes, every time we meet you ask about my day and I tell you. But I realised I don't know anything about you. I think that's a bit rude on my part. You should stop me if I always talk about myself.'

'I like listening to you.'

'I love meeting up with you once a week, but don't you have any other friends?'

'Milly, I enjoy seeing you too and, to be honest, I don't mix with a lot of people. So you're highly honoured to spend time with me.'

'Okay.' Milly isn't perturbed. 'Do you have family?'

'Not now. I was an only child and my parents died in a car accident three years ago.'

Milly's hand shoots up to cover her mouth. 'Oh, no, me and my big mouth.'

'Don't worry. I miss them but I'm fine on my own. I'd been in Manchester for four years and they were still in Dorset. I barely saw them unless it was Christmas or a birthday.'

'Did you live by the sea?' Milly changes the subject as only a teenager can do.

'We were about ten minutes' walk.'

'Cool, so you went there a lot?'

'Most weekends and summer evenings when the nights were light.'

'And what about relationships?'

I laugh. 'You're rather nosy today, aren't you?'

'Sorry! I blame that on my age.' Milly leans forward and whispers. 'Have you ever been in love?'

Love? I'm beginning to think Milly might have a crush on me. I hope not but I humour her.

'Once. I was with someone for two years but it didn't work out in the end.'

'Oh, that's a shame. Where did you meet?'

'At the rowing club.'

'Rowing club?'

'Yes, I used to go out on the sea.'

'Wow!' Milly sits waiting for me to continue, but I say nothing. 'And?' she says impatiently.

'We knew each other from school and got together at a party there. That's why we grew apart, I think. Everything and everyone in our past was too similar. It was a small circle. Have you ever had a boyfriend?'

Milly blushes as she shakes her head.

'Ever kissed anyone?'

'I had a Christmas kiss once but it only lasted about five seconds. I thought he'd done it for a bet and that I'd get teased by Jaimie.'

'And you didn't follow it up?'

'What do you mean?'

'Did he kiss you again?'

'Oh, no. He avoided me after that.'

I stare at her, and she looks away momentarily.

*

I think about what Milly said as I get into bed this evening, and more to the point what she hasn't said about Jaimie. There's more going on than she's telling me, I am sure.

If truth be known, I really like Milly; our friendship has grown stronger week by week. I know it's wrong but I won't take advantage of her.

And at least now I have something I can do for her.

DAY 4

16 August 2019

CHAPTER TWENTY-THREE

Alex

I turn the sound up on the TV while I wipe myself with a towel. I do a workout most mornings before leaving the house, hoping to rid myself of the pent-up anger and emotions I feel all the time.

The people in the video are super fit. The men all muscles and six-packs. The women all tits, arse and big lips. What is it with women who think having big lips is sexy? It's nothing but false, that stupid trout pout. And don't get me started on the narcissistic facelifts and Botoxed foreheads. Nature intended women to look old and saggy at the appropriate age. Why fight against it? It's vanity gone mad.

Mind, I always think people who want to look different aren't happy with themselves for some reason. It's the same with me. As a teenager, I suffered from bulimia but I never told anyone, as it wasn't the done thing to admit. I know it's odd for someone like me at my age but I still do it now, if truth be told. I'll get the urge after a meal to stick two fingers down my throat to bring it all up again. It feels good to purge, like I'm in charge. And I have to be in control when there are other things to think about.

Having Eva here gives me a goal, a purpose, if you like, not to do it. To stay on the straight and narrow until this is over. I'm sure I'll manage it, unless I have a minor relapse. Sometimes even the sight of food can start me off, which is why I only have my favourite things when I know I can get to the bathroom as quickly as possible to get rid of it. It's such a weird condition to have but I'm used to it now. I couldn't cope with being anorexic. I need my strength to do what I do. I have to stay strong.

My temper has got much worse over the past few months, and it's lucky for Eva that I do things to keep calm, or I might take it out on her. Sometimes the need to lash out is so strong that I can't control it. Maxine got the brunt of it once or twice. She was the noisiest of all the women, insisting on banging and screaming whenever she could. The new neighbour from next door once came around and asked me to turn down my TV. I apologised for the noise and went to sort Maxine out. She didn't make a noise again, not after I'd finished with her.

But I don't like taking my annoyance out on the women. I prefer to be cruel in other ways. It's really demeaning to be locked in that room, with no one to talk to, hardly any food, no fresh air and clean clothes. All the luxuries that we take for granted.

Eva seems to be settling in quite well. To my knowledge, she hasn't made a lot of noise. I've heard her banging once or twice, but it hasn't been enough to get anyone else's attention.

I smile as I think of Milly calling round last week. Of course, I hardly ever tell her anything that is true. It's so easy to make lies up, and if I had a lot of friends it might be a problem recalling what I'd said to who. I remember once telling Milly all about my relationship. Well, the made-up version. I was sad when it ended but it had been for the best. It wasn't what I needed. I still haven't found that and I'm not sure I ever will.

But someone will take care of me eventually.

It's what I deserve.

CHAPTER TWENTY-FOUR

Eva

Eva woke up feeling groggy again. She wiped at her eyes with the cuff of her sweatshirt, repelled that she wasn't wearing her own clothes. Hating that he had stripped her to get her undressed. Detesting everything about him.

And yet she wanted to see him. She desperately wanted to talk to someone after so long in here. The loneliness, the isolation was getting to her. She wasn't sure she could make it through another week. That was if she ever got out of here at all.

She sat up, hoping the nausea would be gone today, but as a fresh wave of dizziness swept through her, she was running across to the bucket again. Afterwards, she wiped her mouth with the sleeve of her sweatshirt, already stained from the day before. She crawled to the mattress and sat with her back to the wall, looking at the door.

She thought back to how she'd been feeling over the past four days. Sure the food was enough to make anyone sick. Cheese spread sandwiches on cheap white bread, and milky tea with a bitter taste because she knew it contained some sort of sedative.

She'd been tired, having cramps, but she'd put that down to the lack of food.

She'd felt hot and dizzy, but she'd put that down to the lack of air in the room.

She'd been in an agitated state of stress, but that was to be expected.

Yet, she now realised it wasn't the situation that was making her ill. She'd missed her period last month and had been keeping everything crossed since.

She suspected she might be pregnant. And it broke her heart as much as it made it sing.

Why did this have to happen now?

She pictured Nick's face as she told him the news. He'd sweep her up in his arms, delighted by the fact he was going to be a dad. She would smile and they would kiss and hug, and then keep it to themselves until she was a little further gone. When it was safe to announce, they would tell Nick's family and their friends. Everyone would be happy for them too.

And then she pictured herself with a large bump, Nick's hand pressed to it. Tears of joy and frustration mingled into one. Of course, she'd need to have a test but she was as certain as she could be. She wanted to be pregnant so much, but she knew it was risky right now. With hardly any food and drink, she could ruin her chances of it anyway.

She rested on the mattress again, a hand on her stomach, wondering, hoping, begging. She couldn't cope with the thought of losing a precious opportunity because she was trapped in here. But at least she had a reason to get out, something to aim for.

Someone to look after.

JULY 2019

CHAPTER TWENTY-FIVE

Stoke News

Police Officer Missing in Stoke-on-Trent
Eva Farmer, Senior News Reporter
17 July 2019

Staffordshire Police are gravely concerned over the disappearance of Jillian Bradshaw. Jillian, 42, a police officer, failed to return from a scheduled meeting with a member of the public. When colleagues arrived at the address she was visiting, they found the property empty.

Husband Steve, 44, also a serving police officer, said, 'I spoke to Jill that morning and she seemed fine to me. There was nothing to suggest she was in danger. I don't know what to think, except for the possibility that if someone is holding her, she will be set free in ten days. Her children miss her dearly – I do too. I'm trying not to fear the worst.'

DC Bradshaw is on compassionate leave, having been removed from the case while further investigations take place.

DCI Stan Hedley, Senior Investigating Officer, said, 'We're looking into this abduction and can conclude that we are linking Jillian's disappearance to recent abductions of three women, all from within the Staffordshire areas.

'Stephanie Harvey, 36, was abducted in January; 66-year-old Maxine Stallington was abducted on 12 March; Alison Green, 39, went missing on 15 May. As yet all links we've found have turned out to be inconclusive.

'Mrs Bradshaw has two older children who are worried about her too. It's very distressing and we are working with the four families, as well as monitoring all channels and following up leads from the general public.

'We urge everyone to think what they were doing around the time Jillian Bradshaw went missing on 15 July, and to contact us if they can think of anything, no matter how trivial, and get in touch with us on the helpline printed below.'

CHAPTER TWENTY-SIX

Jillian Bradshaw

Jillian couldn't believe she'd been careless enough to be captured. She knew her abductor had been clever to stay under their radar for so long. Her team had no idea who he was. There had been no sightings of him. And each MO had been different.

She reckoned it was only a matter of time before he messed up though. It was just frustrating being one of his victims and also knowing that she'd slipped up.

But had she? That was the thing – she couldn't remember.

As she suspected the other women had probably done, she tried to count down the days to her release. At least then she could get out of here and tell her colleagues what she knew. Which, quite frankly, wasn't much more than they already knew anyway.

Jill had sat with all three women who had been abducted before her. Through her job as a police officer, she'd spoken to them and their families, worked with her team trying to figure out a link to each one and, just as they'd thought they were getting close, this had happened.

Abducting her too meant it definitely had to be someone connected to the women's vocations. But in their professions, they worked with so many people that it was hard to find the one link between them all. Yet even without her, Jill knew everyone would be working hard to find out who he was.

The room was stifling and she was thirsty again. One bottle of water was all she was allowed each day, and she tried to ration it as much as she could. To her reckoning, she was on day seven now. She'd memorised everything she could: the sounds inside the house, the noises outside on the street. The gait of his feet.

It was the knowing she couldn't get out until he released her that was the worst thing. That and the stench of the place. The stench of her. She smelled disgusting.

She could tell from talking to the women that this was the place he took them to. She just wished they'd had more leads. She couldn't even get him to talk to her. All she saw was that grabber coming through.

She'd tried to kick him through the hatch, but she'd only managed to get his head before he'd moved back. He'd punished her then and, after a day without food or drink, her survival instinct had kicked in, her police training too. Since then she'd thought it best to keep him onside.

It was amazing how the mind played tricks on her now she was shut away from the world. But all she could focus on was getting back to reality. Her home, her family, her job. That was if she even wanted to continue being a police officer after she'd let her guard down.

Or at least she thought she had.

It was a pity it wasn't a fair fight. She couldn't do anything stuck in there, nothing to her advantage. But he may let his guard down one night, and she would be waiting. Because mentally she was fit enough. With an end game of ten days, she could do this.

Yet there were times she realised she was slipping. It was tough mentally not to see or speak to anyone for so long. So much so she wondered if she'd lose the ability to speak once she was outside again. Although she did talk to herself during the day, to ward off the sense of loneliness.

Jill didn't know what to think any more about why he was doing this, to her and those other women. He was just a nameless, faceless creep. A coward.

A real man would stand forward and be counted, not do something secretively. But she wasn't going to antagonise him by saying that. She wanted to go home, so she was going to play the game.

Tears fell again and she wiped at her eyes, the cuff on the grey sweatshirt dirty from doing it so often. She missed her family. She missed everything about her life, but she continually thought about it all to keep her going. People would be missing her too. People would be looking for her.

He wouldn't grind her down. She was strong. This would not faze her. She would get out of this and catch the bastard. She'd make it her mission not to stop until she did. Or until her mind slipped into thoughts of hopelessness.

APRIL 2019

CHAPTER TWENTY-SEVEN

Alex

I've been studying Jaimie's routine for over two weeks now, figuring out the optimum time to pounce. And now it's nearly here.

While I wait, I think of Milly. I fume inwardly, recalling what she's told me about Jaimie. Bullies are wimps when it comes to standing up to someone better than themselves. They pick on the weak and I hate them for it. So now is the time to have a word in someone's ear.

As regular as clockwork, Jaimie comes out of the coffee shop. She says goodbye to her friends and begins the short journey to her home.

I follow closely behind, making sure she doesn't notice me. It's dark now, but I'm all dressed in black, with trainers so there'll be no noise. Jaimie has her phone in her hand as she walks. I know where she's heading so I don't have to keep up with her. I stay far enough away that she doesn't know she's being followed.

As she turns into a street that I know will be quiet, I run up behind her, grabbing her around the neck and holding a knife to the side of her face.

'Don't make a fucking sound,' I mutter, my breath close to the girl's face. 'Such a shame if anything happens to you near your

100 of their lives. Not you, though, because you'll be dead.'

home. Your parents will have to live with that memory for the rest of their lives. Not you, though, because you'll be dead.'

Jaimie whimpers.

'I'm a bigger bully than you and, believe me, you don't want to make me angry.' I pull on her neck so my grip is tighter. 'Do you hear?'

The girl tries to nod, then speaks. 'Yes.'

'There's a good girl. Now, what I want you to do is behave yourself when you're at school. I've heard a lot of things about you being nasty to some of the other kids. It stops, right now. Give me your phone.'

'Wh-what?'

I hold out my hand. 'Give me your phone.'

'I… no.'

'Have you just listened to a word I said? Give me your fucking phone.'

The girl passes it back to me.

'See, that wasn't too hard, was it? I'm taking this with me. Don't think blocking it will be of any use, as I have equipment to bypass that. I'm going to retrieve and store all your photos and contacts. I've been following you, Jaimie. I know all about your rendezvous with that poncy boy you've been hanging around with. If you mess with me, I'll take both of your faces and superimpose them onto some entirely different photos. And then I'll send them to everyone you know. They won't be very flattering, do you understand?'

Jaimie's knees buckle underneath her. I keep my grip on her firm.

'Quite frankly, I'm doing you a favour,' I go on. 'If you start being kind to people now, then you'll get on better in life. Stop being a spoiled bitch and start acting like a respectable person. And don't even think for a moment of telling your parents or the police about my threat.'

The girl's crying now.

'It isn't pleasant being the underdog, is it? Just remember this is how you make people feel. And if you ever, ever lay another finger on anyone else, I will be back to rip off your head. I know where you live. Now, piss off before I get even more angry.'

I release the girl and push her forwards. She falls, landing on her knees, but gets up quickly. She doesn't even look back as she runs away. But I can hear her sobs.

I watch until she is out of sight and then turn to go home. Of course, I know she'll tell her parents and they'll contact the police. But I doubt Jaimie will say why I threatened her. I'm sure it will be chalked up to another faceless mugging.

Only the two of us will know the truth.

DAY 4

16 August 2019

CHAPTER TWENTY-EIGHT

Alex

Work is becoming a bit of a bind now, but I have to stick to the plan and act normal. Yet I do wonder if it's worth this being my last day here, as I can't concentrate. It's not that stressful at the office really but I can't wait to leave. It's my final day soon, regardless of how I'm feeling. I've booked next week off and after that I'll be gone, once I've got what I want and removed that bitch out of my life for good.

I sense someone standing in front of me. I look up and see the man from accounts. He's worked here as long as me and yet he never addresses me by my name. I know his but I'm not going to use it just to spite him. Invisible, no talk other than what's necessary.

'Can you check my computer?' he asks.

'Have you logged a job?'

'No, I thought I'd come and see you on the off chance you can squeeze me in. You're not busy, are you?'

I sigh inwardly. Sure I don't have anything better to do as I fit in work for everyone else. Who was I lining up lunch with anyway? I'm a nobody here.

'I have a report that needs to be finished by tomorrow,' he adds. 'I was working on it yesterday and now I can't find it.'

I push myself to my feet and follow him to his desk. The job doesn't take long. The idiot has hidden the document somewhere he's forgotten about. Of course, he's denied that, but I can see for myself. I'm not stupid, even if he thinks I am.

I let him prattle on and then I leave him to it. He doesn't even say thank you, just starts typing away. I've a good mind to log in to his computer from the main server and delete his report. Yes, I'll do that, but only once he's worked on it some more. That will teach him.

In front of my desk again, the ticker tape runs across the TV with Eva's details on it, the screen flashing up photos of her every fifteen minutes. Everyone is working hard to find her.

It seems strange to see her all the time. It makes me laugh to think no one around me knows she's in my cellar. It's such a buzz.

The police have started to link the women now. There are pictures of all of them – Stephanie, Maxine, Alison and Jillian. Sometimes when I see their faces, I get so pissed off. Other times, it's hard for me not to start grinning. Their fate was in my hands – still is, really, but they don't know my plans.

The afternoon passes and I collect today's copy of the *Stoke News* on my way home. I'm thinking about what to cook for my supper tonight. I might call in at the supermarket when I get off the bus and grab a ready meal, and a bottle of red to go with it. There's no point in doing a big shop now.

Still, it won't be long before everything is out in the open. In a weird way, I'm quite looking forward to it. It's been hard keeping it to myself over the years. And besides, I'm doing it for Jude too. He'd be pleased about it all. I know he would. I still feel him near regardless. I guess we'll never lose that bond.

CHAPTER TWENTY-NINE

Eva

Eva was sitting on the bed, her fingers tapping on the side of her thigh. The thought of being pregnant had left her in an agitated state. Her stress levels had rocketed, her chest hurting as her breathing became laboured. She'd tried walking around to calm herself but it had made her feel claustrophobic, to the point that she'd banged on the door for several minutes. She had to do something or she was going to go stir crazy and have a full-on panic attack, which wouldn't be wise at all.

Spent, she'd slept for a while but hunger pains had woken her. She'd cried and then she'd been thinking some more. In the end, she came to the conclusion that she wouldn't reveal her pregnancy unless it was absolutely necessary and she was in danger. He could use it against her. He could hit her again and make her miscarry.

It was so hot, she could see a vivid blue sky out of the window; she longed to feel the air outside and the heat on her skin in an uncontrolled environment. Sweat was pouring from her, her own body odour making her retch. The whole room stank of stale air.

Finally, she heard the front door open. She listened to footsteps upstairs for several minutes and then the door to the stairs open.

She dropped to the floor behind the hatch. Inside her head, she counted his footsteps down the stairs. Eight, nine, ten, eleven. Then four more across to the door. She heard the key going into the padlock and the sound of the bolt being pulled across.

The hatch opened and she waited until the tray was pushed through. She was about to reach for the newspaper when, instead, she grabbed for what she could. She touched skin, wrapped her fingers around a wrist and pulled with all her might, until she could grip it more forcefully.

'Let me out of here!' she screamed.

There was a muffle as she continued to pull. She put a foot either side of the door and heaved. She wasn't sure what she was going to do but she wanted to hurt him, twist his hand round, perhaps break it. She wouldn't be able to get out but, right now, she would take great satisfaction in hurting him.

'Talk to me, you bastard,' she cried, her grip tightening, fingers digging in.

'Get off me!'

Eva was so surprised to hear the voice that she let go immediately. When she realised her error, she reached out again, but it was too late. The hatch was slammed shut and she was on her own once more.

She moved forward and put her ear closer to the door, wondering if she'd heard right. But there was silence.

'I'm sorry!' She slapped her palm on the door. 'I promise I won't hurt you again. I just want to speak to someone, to see you. I can't stay in here—'

'You've spoiled everything now,' the voice interrupted.

'I just want to talk to you. Who are you?'

'You really want to know?'

'Yes.'

There was a long pause. 'I'm Witness1575.'

Eva froze. At first she'd thought her ears were playing tricks on her. And yet, even now, she still couldn't believe it.

Because she knew exactly who was holding her captive.

And Witness1575 was female.

FEBRUARY 2007

CHAPTER THIRTY

Stoke News

Man and Woman Jailed for the Murder of Ten-year-old Boy
Eva Farmer, Senior News Reporter
16 February 2007

A mother and her partner who horrifically abused ten-year-old twins were sent to prison today. The couple from Longton, who cannot be named to protect the identity of the surviving child, kept the children locked in their bedroom and when one of them suffered an injury, he was left to bleed to death, despite his sister screaming out for help. The tragic youngster died from a ruptured spleen that was left unattended for at least twelve hours. His sibling, known as Witness1575, gave evidence by video.

The man, 36, was sentenced to fifteen years for manslaughter and the woman, 32, who was the twins' mother, received eleven years. Neither are expected to get parole until their full sentences have been served.

The boy died on 22 August 2006. The court heard that when paramedics were called to the property, they found the deceased and immediately called the police. They also noticed a lock was fitted to the exterior of the children's bedroom door.

Jailing the couple, his Honour Judge Horrock said, 'I was saddened and sickened by what you put the children through. They were in your care, looking to you for love, food and comfort, and yet all you did was torture them, as if they were a burden. Shame on you.

'When the jury first saw the photographs of the condition in which the boy had died, they must have wondered how you would explain what had gone on. All you did was tell lies and ignore the reality of the offence, to try and get a lesser sentence for yourself. You both should have known better.'

During the three-week trial, the man claimed he did not realise the extent of the injuries caused to the boy. The woman expressed her innocence several times, claiming she was a victim too. But the jury found them both guilty of the charges brought against them, taking only four hours to convict the pair.

Speaking after the case, Detective Inspector Noelle Wilkins, of Staffordshire Police, said, 'The investigation involved taking evidence from a young child who was asked to recall traumatic and distressing events from their past, recounting details of horrific psychological and emotional abuse.'

Witness 1575 was moved into the care of the local authority.

DAY 4

16 August 2019

CHAPTER THIRTY-ONE

Eva

Eva stepped backwards until her feet hit the mattress and she collapsed onto it. Everyone, including her, had thought the abductor was a man. No one had jumped to the conclusion – in a lot of meetings and reports it had been stated the abductor was *someone*, no set gender because no one had been seen.

The level of violence and intimidation seemed to suit as well. To her mind, there was no indication it would be a woman. The other abductees talked about a man. Or were there two of them – a man and a woman? She shook her head, trying to work everything out. Could that really be Witness1575 out there?

As a young reporter, the Carrington/Dixon case had been the biggest Eva had worked on. She cast her mind back to going to the court with the editor-in-chief. She'd been obsessed with the case, or rather the surviving child getting justice, and she did everything she could to find out more about the young witness. Eva had seen the girl once or twice in the court rooms, flanked by social workers and police officers that she didn't know. She'd spoken to her on one occasion but, more often than not, all she heard was a girl's voice coming from a video call.

The case had been headline news for quite some time. How Ian Carrington had locked two children away in a room while their mother, Maria Dixon, went to work.

That fateful summer, it had escalated at the end of the school holidays to the point where Maria suffered at his hands too. According to her testimonial, she was threatened if she spoke to her children and beaten if she let them out of their room. Eva recalled the judge saying she should have found the courage to get away with them, but after seeing what happened to her own mother when she was a child, she knew it wasn't that simple. Maria Dixon had probably lived in fear of her own life too.

Eva stood up and paced the room as she tried to make sense of it all. What did the woman want with Eva now? Was she after some kind of revenge? And if so, why her? So many questions ran through her mind.

The case had given Eva sleepless nights for months, before and after the trial. It had been splashed across the media for three weeks. Everyone knew that Carrington and Dixon were guilty, and despite their pleas that neither of them were at fault, the jury had decided otherwise and they'd received the sentences they deserved.

Eva had kept abreast of the couple for a few years afterwards; she knew that Carrington had been beaten to death while in prison after serving only two years of his sentence. To her, that didn't seem long enough for what he'd done.

She had never forgotten Witness1575, and had often wondered if the girl found happiness, a new family, a new life. Eva didn't know what to think about that right now.

She sat, listening. The silence was loaded.

A few minutes later, the hatch was unlocked and opened again.

Eva moved across to it. 'Please. Will you speak to me?' she asked.

'I suppose it won't hurt. But not yet. I need to think.'

The hatch closed with a bang and Eva heard the woman leaving. She thought back to that ten-year-old girl being brave enough to give evidence against the people who had killed her twin brother, one of them a blood relative. People who should have kept them both safe from harm.

To her reckoning, Witness1575 would be twenty-three now. And she would be the clear link between the four women who were abducted before her. Each one of them could have come into contact with Witness1575 as part of their jobs. She would also be a link to Eva herself, as she had reported the case to the *Stoke News*.

She would need to think about why their captor wanted to harm women who had supported her. Now she knew who she was dealing with, she wondered if she could play up to that emotion.

CHAPTER THIRTY-TWO

Alex

Yes, that's me – Witness1575. I'm surprised everyone thought I was a man. I mean, come on. Women can be just as vicious when it comes to getting revenge. It's the reason I train hard with weights. I'm only medium build but I pack a mean punch when someone is drugged.

I know you think I'm callous but these women ruined my life. Every one of them. So I kidnap them and then let them go after ten days, to show them what it's like to be invisible. To have no one to talk to; to have no one to love you. It's not a nice place to be. I should know.

I'm so tired of my life and I hate living like this, knowing I will always want to hurt people. Yet *people* need to know. My story needs to be told.

But Eva. She's trying to spoil it for me. Why would she grab me like that, when she knows she can't get away? What a stupid thing to do.

And now she knows who I am.

I pace around the kitchen, adrenaline pulsing through me, while I try to get my thoughts in order. I am shocked, so I sit for a few minutes.

And then it all becomes clear. My plan can be adapted. I'll change things to accommodate her knowing who I am. Well, who I was, anyway.

I have more purpose now. She has to do something for me before I will let her go. She will have to be willing too. Because if she isn't keen, there is only one alternative.

This will work out better than I'd imagined now. I have six days to talk to Eva, get to know her and then she can do what she needs to do, which is tell my story. Although, I have given way too much away during that conversation.

I've had a neat shot of whisky, and I find I like the idea of speaking to Eva. Apart from Milly, it's been a long time since I've had someone to talk to.

A friend. That's what I will become. To fool Eva. I can win her over.

I smile as I fling myself onto the sofa, crossing my legs at the ankles. Perhaps this will turn out better than I'd hoped. I reach for my notepad and list items I want to discuss with Eva. It's all up to her, how long I keep her, and whether I let her go after ten days or not, although I prefer to stick to the original plan. And once Eva has typed out my story, I will leave it, and her, where it will be seen. But not too obvious a place because I want to be long gone by then.

Or I might even release her before the ten days are up. Leave her somewhere she won't be found so easily. That would fool everyone.

The power I have is incredible.

Yes, I need to let Eva believe I'm playing into her hands. I have the whole world at my fingertips. No one knows where I am, that much is clear. And this house is perfect for what I have planned.

Because I'm not going anywhere yet. Eva is going to tell everyone my life story. And I know exactly how it will end.

And when.

2006

CHAPTER THIRTY-THREE

Alex

January 2006

We didn't have a very nice Christmas this year. Ian got drunk all the time and became nasty.

We don't like Ian. He's our mum's new boyfriend. They've been together for a few months now. Mum told us she was lonely after Dad died. She said she'd met someone nice and he would look after us all. But he doesn't seem to like me and Jude. He does mean things to us when Mum isn't around. He makes us play in our room and not come out. I like my brother and, even though we are twins, I don't want to be with him all the time and he doesn't want to be with me. So it's hard when we have to play together for such a long time. We start falling out. And when we're together we can be really noisy. Ian doesn't like that either.

Mum has changed too. When Dad was alive, she used to smile and laugh a lot. But now she doesn't. She seems really scared of Ian. Me and Jude know that he hits her, as we can hear it when we are in bed. They argue and shout a lot when Ian comes in from the pub. We hear Mum crying all the time. I wish Ian would leave and it would be just me, Mum and Jude again. Even if Dad can't come back, it would be better without Ian.

I miss my dad. I know Jude misses him too. We talk about him a lot when we're on our own. We talk about things we used to do, the places we used to go. The time Dad took us to the zoo and fell into the penguin enclosure. The holidays in Devon. Camping in the rain, and then in a caravan. We had so many adventures.

It was horrible that Dad died so quickly. We were eight when it happened. He had cancer. One minute he was fine and the next he was poorly, and he never recovered.

I wish he was still alive. If he was, Ian wouldn't be living with us and we would still be a happy family. Since Ian has moved in with us, we have to be quiet or else he clips us around the head. Even if we're being good, he'll do that sometimes too. We don't like him but we don't tell anyone that. We just try to behave as much as we can. But we're ten years old and kids are meant to be noisy. Well, we are anyway.

February 2006

It's half-term and it's been a long day. Mum has been at work and rang to find us on our own. Ian went out a while ago and we've been having fun without him. Mum is angry that he left, so as a treat she nipped to the chippie at the end of the street on her way home.

'Mum's here!' I shout to Jude, and we come flying into the kitchen almost as one.

'Did you get us mushy peas?' Jude asks as he rummages through the carrier bag.

'Let me get through the door first, you monster.' Mum laughs.

I laugh too. It's not often that Mum smiles these days, let alone giggles along with us. I miss it. But when it is just the three of us, it's much more fun.

We help Mum dish out the food, plating up something for Ian who should be home soon. I hope he stays out long enough for us to enjoy the chips together. But we have barely started eating when we hear the front door open.

We were chatting away before he stepped into the kitchen, but we know we have to be quiet now. He doesn't even look at us. He stares at our mum as he shuffles around the table.

'Where's mine?' He pulls out a chair and sits down.

Mum gets to her feet immediately and retrieves it from the oven.

I eat my food quietly, staring at Jude. At first he isn't looking at me, but when he catches my eye, I cross mine and pull a face. He laughs, some of his food spilling out of his mouth.

'What the hell's wrong with you?' Ian roars. 'Behave while you're at the table.'

'It was her fault,' Jude says. 'She made me laugh.'

'I did not,' I cry, but then I burst into laughter.

'Enough,' Ian shouts.

'They're only messing around, Ian,' Mum says. 'We all love a chippie tea. It's a special treat.'

'Is that so?' Ian's face darkens and, in one swoop, he swipes my plate off the table. Jude's follows and then he glares at Mum before knocking hers to the floor too.

'Oh, Ian,' Mum says.

Ian swipes his hand across her mouth. Then all hell breaks loose as we try to stop him from hitting her again. I scream as loud as I can. Jude holds one of Ian's arms, and Mum tries to get out of the kitchen.

'Get to your room, you pair of imbeciles,' Ian seethes.

I can see the veins popping at the side of his head. It's very scary.

'But we haven't eaten anything,' Jude protests.

'I said get out of my sight!'

We don't need telling again. I look at the food all over the floor. It smells so good, and the few chips I've dipped into my mushy peas had tasted so nice. Now Mum will have to clean it all up, and she's in trouble with Ian. I hope he doesn't hit her again, as it's all my fault.

Mum follows us into the hall as we scoot upstairs. 'Stay in your room and don't come out until I say,' she whispers. 'I'll try and bring you some toast if he goes to the pub later.'

But Ian doesn't go out. Instead he argues and shouts at Mum for the rest of the evening. Me and Jude stay in our room. We are hungry but there is nothing we can do about it. We'll have to stay upstairs until the morning now.

'Why did you make me laugh?' Jude asks later as we lie in the dark.

'I'm sorry. I couldn't help it. I was excited.'

'About what?'

'Having chips for tea. Seeing Mum laughing and joking with us before he came home.'

'I wish he didn't live here with us.'

'Me too. I hate him.'

'He's an ass.'

'He's a bastard.'

Jude gasps and then starts to giggle. Before long we are both laughing uncontrollably again. There is a bang on the door and we jump. We quieten down. There is no point trying to go downstairs until the morning. If we settle down now, he might not hurt Mum too much.

I miss my dad. I miss him so much. He wouldn't allow this to happen. He would have been around to look after us. He wouldn't have left us alone to go to the pub. I hate Ian. I really do.

April 2006

As soon as we get in from school, Ian makes us go to our bedroom and he doesn't let us out. There's no lock on the door, so we can go to the bathroom but that's it. He isn't even going to the pub now, so we are trapped.

It's quite boring at times, so entertaining ourselves is the only thing we can do. Now we're playing at being jungle animals. I'm an orangutang and Jude is a lion.

'Roarrrrr,' Jude cries as we race from one corner of the room to another. I shriek and make monkey noises. We are being so loud that we don't hear the footsteps before it's too late.

'What the hell is going on in here?' Ian shouts from the hallway.

I hear someone on the landing and freeze, looking at Jude in dismay. We're in for it now.

The door flings open, crashing into the wall.

'Sorry,' we speak in unison and run to sit on our beds.

But our apologies aren't going to be enough. 'You will have no food for the rest of the day,' Ian says.

I hold in a sob. We haven't eaten since last night, and all we had then was a slice of cold toast to share.

'Please, Ian,' I plead with him. 'It was my fault. I was the one being noisy. Don't punish Jude as well.'

'It wasn't you,' Jude replies, prodding himself in the chest. 'It was me. It was my fault.'

'Well, aren't you the two loyal dogs?' Ian laughs, his face contorting in mirth. Then he strides across the room towards us, grabbing both of us by our hair. He pulls us to our feet as we cry out in pain.

'Either you shut the fuck up or I'll do something to guarantee you won't make a noise for a good while. Do you hear?'

'Yes, Ian,' we answer.

He releases his grip, pushing us away. 'If I hear one more peep,' he says quietly, holding up his index finger, 'you will know it.'

We sit in silence, looking at the floor. Ian turns and walks out, slamming the door shut.

We both let out our breath.

'I hate him,' Jude whispers.

'I do too,' I whisper back. 'But we won't be here forever. One day we'll be big enough to do what we want.'

It isn't a good answer but it's the only one I have.

*

Today, a bolt is fitted to the outside of our bedroom door.

July 2006

School holidays. Six whole weeks off. I know a lot of my friends are looking forward to it. Some are going to the seaside in this country. Some are going on an aeroplane and flying out to places like Spain and Cyprus.

But me and Jude aren't looking forward to the summer break at all. Because Ian is around. He's lost his job now so he'll be stuck with us all day. We won't be able to have any fun. We won't be able to make a noise. It's not fair.

'I'm so sticky,' I say to Jude, who is looking out of the window at a clear blue sky. 'I wish we could have a paddling pool and be able to go out in the garden.'

'Yeah.' Jude points to the yard. 'It's not fair that we have to stay in all day. We should tell Mum that he locks us in our rooms while she's at work.'

'We can't do that.' I panic. 'It will make him worse.'

'But we need to get out of here. If he doesn't let us out, I'm going to climb through the window. See how he likes that.'

I laugh. There is no way Jude can get down to the ground floor without hurting himself. But then I see Jude is serious. 'You can't. It's too high.'

'I can tell someone what's happening then.'

'Who's going to believe us? He'll say we're lying.'

Jude turns his back on me then. 'It's not right that we're locked in here. It's the big holidays. I'm going to tell Mum when she comes in.'

'She won't do anything about it. She's scared of him. He's a horrible man.'

I sit on my bed, arms folded. I have had enough of Ian telling us what to do all the time. 'He isn't our dad,' I say. 'I'm going to knock on the door until he lets us out.'

'No, don't do that.'

'Watch me.'

I reach for the book by the side of my bed. It's a hardback. I jump up and go over to the door. 'Ian, let us out!' I shout, banging the book's spine on the door.

'Stop it! You'll get us in trouble.'

'I want old Mrs Martin to hear us.' Mrs Martin is our neighbour, who lives in the house next door. 'She'll tell someone and we'll be let out.' I bang on the door again. 'Ian!' I shout. 'Let us out.'

I hear him thundering up the stairs. The door is unlocked and he's in the room.

'What the hell do you want now?' he yells.

I notice he's swaying. I put my hand across my face as he comes towards me. He smells like Grandad Dixon did before he died. Mum said he was an alcoholic. Ian smells like that too.

'We want to play in the garden.' I fold my arms defiantly.

'Oh, you do, do you?' Ian folds his arms too. 'I don't want you out of this room until your mum comes back from work. And even then, I might not let you out. Because you're so bloody noisy.'

Jude makes a run for the door, but Ian is too quick. He grabs his arm, squeezing tightly.

Jude cries out.

'Where do you think you're going?' Ian says.

'I want to go to the toilet. I've been dying to go for ages.'

'You can both wait until your mum gets back.'

'I need to go now.'

'Well, piss your pants.'

'I can't.' Jude is crossing his legs and dancing.

'That's not fair,' I say. 'If he's quiet, he could use the bathroom and be back quickly.'

Ian rolls his eyes and groans. 'What did I tell you? You can wait.'

'But I—'

He swaps his grip on Jude to grab my arm next. I can feel his fingers digging into my flesh and I squeal.

'Come with me,' he says and pulls me out of the room.

'Let her go,' Jude cries, coming over to us.

'You stay there!' Ian barks.

He drags me downstairs to the kitchen. He's hurting my arm and I cry out. He pushes me into a chair and searches through the drawers until he finds what he's looking for. He holds up a pair of scissors.

'I'll give you something to moan about, you stupid girl.'

He takes hold of my hair and before I can react, he's hacking at it, as close to my head as he can get. I watch as my long blonde hair falls to the floor.

'Stop!' I cry out in pain.

He grabs more and cuts another chunk. I try to push him away but he's too strong. He hacks at my hair again two more times and then he stops and eyes his handiwork. He laughs in my face. 'Do you want me to continue?'

I shake my head fervently.

'Well then, until your mother gets in, you'll be quiet, do you hear?'

I nod as I sob quietly. I hate him.

'Get out of my sight.'

I run upstairs, back to our room, and throw myself onto the bed. I don't want to look at Jude. I don't want him to see my hair. I must look horrid.

'Mum will be back soon,' Jude whispers as he comes to sit next to me.

'She won't do anything,' I reply. 'She's scared of Ian too.'

Jude puts an arm around me, and I cry into his shoulder. Then I curl up on my bed and put my face to the wall. I don't want to look at my hair. It will be such a mess. I hope Ian doesn't take it out on Mum, too, when she gets in.

We don't deserve this. We're kids. We should be able to play and make a noise. We shouldn't be locked in a room all day.

*

This morning, Mum brings us some toast and tea and gives us both a big hug. She tells us to be brave and strong. She says it will be over soon as she is making plans.

August 2006

It's week five of the school holidays. We're good kids, me and Jude. We try to be quiet, locked in the room every day, but we are bored and restless. It is hot again and we can see the sun and wish we were able to play with our friends.

We are fighting when it happens. Jude has a tennis ball and wants me to play catch. I tell him no, but he throws the ball at me anyway and it hits me hard on the leg. In temper I throw it back at him, and it smashes into the lamp at the side of his bed. It crashes to the carpet, bending its flimsy lampshade.

'What's going on up there now?' Ian shouts.

Jude gasps and races over to the lamp, putting it back as Ian unbolts the door. He flies to his bed, grabs a book and pretends to read.

Ian comes hurtling in like a train. 'I said what's going on?' His hands rest on either side of the door frame as he glares from one to the other.

'Nothing,' Jude says.

Ian continues to stare at us and then he turns to leave. But he spots the state of the lamp. He points to it and looks at Jude. 'Did you do that?'

'It was an accident.'

Ian drags him off his bed. He hits him around his head, and Jude puts his arms up to defend himself.

'Leave him alone,' I scream and jump up from the bed.

Ian swipes his hand across my face, and I fall to the floor. Jude is next to me now, curled up trying to protect himself. Ian is kicking him in the stomach again and again. The last one sends Jude across the room.

'Stop. You're hurting him!' I grab Ian's arm and dig my teeth into it. He yelps and pushes me away, but this time he marches out of the room. I race across to my brother before I hear the bolt being drawn across again.

'Jude, are you okay?' I say, bursting into tears.

He doesn't say anything. He just groans. This time it's me who puts an arm around him for comfort as I lie next to him on the carpet.

Jude is in a bad way. He needs help.

I have been banging on the door all afternoon, shouting to Ian but I think he's gone out. It was my fault again. I am such a stupid girl. I can't behave myself.

I hear Ian come home just before Mum gets in from work and then Ian shouting at her. Mum is trying to get upstairs to see us, but he won't let her. I can hear him hitting her.

Mum doesn't come up to see us. I know she's scared because she didn't come to see us yesterday either. I wish she could get us out of here and away from Ian right now.

But most of all, I wish she could help Jude. Because there is something really wrong with him.

*

When Mum finally comes into our room the next morning, the look of panic on her face when she sees what has happened makes me cry. Ian comes running in, trying to resuscitate Jude, but he is so cold. Ian shouts at me, but he isn't worried about Jude or me; Ian is only concerned that he will be found out and get into trouble. I am glad of that.

My mum cries so much, cuddling Jude. His arm hangs down as she kisses him over and over.

Ian runs out of the room. Mum tells him to call for an ambulance, but he doesn't. I hope the police catch him if he leaves the house. He is a very bad man.

Mum eventually rings for help. The paramedics look over Jude but there is nothing they can do. The police come too. A lady officer takes my hand and we go downstairs. Ian is in the hallway. The police are putting handcuffs on him and saying some words to him that I don't understand.

Before they take him away, he says he is sorry to me. I don't think he means that, really. He's just sorry he is in trouble.

Now I am on my own, as Jude is dead, and I am so scared without him or my mum. What's going to happen to me?

DAY 4

16 August 2019

CHAPTER THIRTY-FOUR

Eva

With Eva's mind still whirring, the woman was back after a short while. The flap was opened and Eva moved closer to it.

'I know you're trying to work out why I abducted you all,' Alex said.

'Well, I would like to know. Seeing as I'm stuck in here and it's down to you,' she countered.

'Don't get arsey with me.'

'Sorry.' Eva bit on her lips, cursing herself for apologising. But at the same time, she was learning how to deal with what she'd discovered about her captor, and if it meant keeping the woman onside, then she'd do whatever it took.

'You have ten days. This is day four. So we can do this your way or mine.'

'What do you want me to do?'

'I have a plan for you. I'm going to tell the world what really happened to me and my brother. I've been following you for years now. I've read most of what you've written and I like your tone.'

'Okay.'

'I also know that you have a tragic family history, so I'm sure you can tell me your story too.'

Eva froze. It seemed the woman had done her research. She never let herself dwell much on her past, hiding her feelings from people. It was part of her life that she didn't want to even think about. It was too painful. But if she had to speak about it, she would. On one condition.

'Can I know your name?' she asked.

'I'll tell you that tomorrow.'

'Why not now?'

'Because I don't feel like it.'

'I might not feel like talking to you then.' Eva chastised herself inwardly as soon as the words were out. She'd spoken without thinking again.

Laughter came through the doorway. 'I don't think you're in any position to tell me what you can or can't do. If you want to eat, that is.'

Eva pushed her fist into her mouth to stop from retaliating. The woman was right: she was the one holding all the cards. Even if it went against every grain in her body, Eva would do as she was told. She had to. Her hand instinctively went to cradle her stomach.

'Okay, tomorrow it is,' Alex replied.

Eva listened as the bolt slid into place, the lock refastened, disappearing footsteps and the slam of a door. Tears dripped down her cheeks even before she'd wrapped herself in the sheet and buried her head underneath it.

Memories of her father were coming back to her. She didn't want to think of him. Not here in this pit. It was punishment enough that she had to stay in it. She didn't want him infiltrating her dreams while she slept.

Four days gone.

Six days more.

That's what she would latch on to. She would think of all the things she'd be able to do and the people she'd be able to see, once she was let out.

Because she *was* going to get out.

DAY 5

17 August 2019

CHAPTER THIRTY-FIVE

Eva

Eva woke with the evil lurch of her stomach as she tried to reach the bucket in time. After vomiting, she lay back on the mattress, her hand resting on her stomach. She didn't have time for angst over the damage she might be causing to the foetus she thought was inside her. She'd been going over what had happened for most of the night, as there had been no sleeping medication administered. Because she'd overstepped the line, she'd been punished and left with no food or drink.

What had she been thinking, throwing herself at the trapdoor and reaching out? Come to think of it, she hadn't been thinking at all. What possible use could it be to grab an arm and pull? The person on the other end wasn't going to magically shrink and squeeze through until they were in the room with her. And what then? She wanted to escape, not be trapped with her abductor. Still, it had proved useful when the woman had shouted out at her.

And that was what she was still trying to get her head around. More than ever, Eva realised she needed to co-operate with her. She couldn't damage the chance of the life growing inside her. Even if the pregnancy hadn't been confirmed, she knew it was there. And she was going to do everything in her power to give her baby the best start in life she could. So if that meant giving in to every demand the woman threw at Eva, then that was what she'd do.

Alongside breakfast, there was a notepad and a pen on the tray that morning. Eva took the toast and bit into it greedily, her shoulders sagging in appreciation. Pregnant or not, she despised feeling so weak-willed by eating the food, but ultimately hated how fragile she was without it. So far this morning alone, she'd been in pain with stomach cramps, hunger pains and had a dry mouth.

'Hurry up and then we can begin,' the woman demanded after a few moments.

Eva couldn't help feeling teary at the sound of another voice. Being locked up in the cellar for so long without speaking to anyone had been agony, and it was so good now to hear the woman talk.

'So I've been thinking and here's what we're going to do,' the woman went on. 'I'm going to tell you about each of my captives, and why I held them here, and you're going to write it all down. Then you will make it into a feature. I'll start at the beginning with Stephanie Harvey. You visited her, didn't you?'

'Yes,' Eva replied.

'Stephanie was my support worker when I was sixteen. She said she'd help me but she didn't.'

Eva swallowed the last of the toast, wiping her hands on the jogging bottoms before speaking again. Then she took up the pen and notepad and began writing.

'In what way was Stephanie supposed to have helped you?' she asked, her journalistic head taking over.

'She said she would find somewhere safe for me to stay when my time in the children's home ran out. She said she'd help me to get a job too. She said both would be a fresh start.'

'But you say she did nothing?' Eva didn't understand.

'Oh, she promised a lot but there was nothing forthcoming. On my sixteenth birthday, I was moved to a hostel for young females. That turned out to be worse than where I'd come from. As if that wasn't bad enough, we weren't supposed to have anyone stopping over, but there were often boys let in at the end of the night.

'During my first week, they broke into my room. They took everything I had, even the little money I'd been given. And they stole the key to the room and wouldn't let me back in. I had to sleep on a chair for a night until I could get help. Then they said I'd grassed them up and I was beaten for reporting them. But I had no choice. How could I survive without a room and no money?'

'How long did you stay there?'

'A couple of months before I legged it. I slept rough until I found a squat. Then I made friends with a girl called Jen. I stayed in her flat for a while, until we fell out.'

Eva was busy writing, but at the same time she was hoping to glean as much information as was possible. She needed to figure out who she was talking to, how to deal with her. How she might have turned into the person she was now.

'Didn't you make any friends at the hostel eventually?' she asked next.

There was a cackle of laughter, its tone cruel and mocking. 'Don't be stupid. I'm the invisible girl. The victim that everyone intended to help but, when it came to it, no one ever did. It was all hearsay and broken promises. "We can do this for you; we can do that for you." But once they left, nothing was done.'

'Did you speak to Stephanie?'

'I showed her the bruising on my face. I told her what had happened and she promised to get me some help. But when I went to see her the next week, she wasn't there. She was ill, they said, and no one else could see me right then. I revisited the following week and found out that she wasn't coming back. She didn't care about me and I-I was left to fend for myself.'

Eva caught up with her notes while she waited for the woman to speak again. She could hear sniffling, as if it was too painful for her to speak. When she did, the anguish was clear in her voice.

'After I let Stephanie go, I saw the article you wrote from her point of view. All the lies she told about how she had no idea who'd be so nasty to her. Of course she didn't remember me. I mean, why would she? I bet no one ever recalls me. As a lonely and vulnerable child, I made myself blend into the background. I didn't want anyone to know who I was, but I could hear them whispering about me once they found out. A child with a murdered brother. A child who was abandoned at ten years old and put into the care of others. Six years I was at the home. And when I was ready to come out, what did Stephanie Harvey do? She abandoned me. I was a closed case: someone else's responsibility. She couldn't wait to get rid of me. So she was the first to feature in my plan.'

Eva was writing as quickly as she could, but was finding it hard to keep up.

'I wanted her to suffer, just like I did. The last day before I set her free, I sat in the room with her. She was feeling really sorry for herself, can you believe that? I drugged her first so she wouldn't recollect anything, but I wanted her to see me, see if she recognised me. I wanted to rip her insides out and show her the damage she'd done. She was supposed to have looked after me, the fucking bitch. So I hit her a few times.'

As the woman's anger intensified, a sense of dread began to build up in Eva at the thought of what could happen to her on day ten if that had been done to Stephanie.

'I'm so sorry no one was there to help you,' she said, ignoring it as much as she could.

'Have you written down what I've said?'

'Yes, I've got most of it.'

'Let me see – and no funny games.'

'But it's—'

'Let me see!'

Eva moved to the hatch and put the notepad on the floor. She slid it through to the other side of the wall. Then she watched as the woman used the grabber to pull it closer to her. She heard the pages turning over. Then suddenly there was a roar that made her jump. The notepad was flung back through the hatch.

'Did I tell you to write in stupid code? I don't know what that says.'

'It's shorthand. I always write that way. I can take down words a lot quicker.'

'But I can't read it.'

'I was going to write it out for you.'

'Too right you will.'

Eva grimaced at the anger in the woman's voice as she told more of the story. But then, suddenly, she heard movement.

'I'm going to have a lie-down. All this talk about my past is making my brain ache.'

Eva didn't want to be alone, not just yet. There was a long day ahead of her if she was left until the evening.

'Wait,' she cried out. 'Don't go yet.'

'You want me to stay and talk to you?'

'Please.' Eva hated the pleading tone in her voice but knew it was necessary. 'You said you'd tell me your name.'

'It's Alex.' She paused. 'And now you know that, Eva, if you want me to stay, you can tell me all about your dad.'

CHAPTER THIRTY-SIX

Eva

Flashbacks of the film *The Silence of the Lambs* flooded Eva's mind in an instant. Young agent Clarice Starling and serial killer Hannibal Lecter. Lecter quizzing Starling about her dad. Starling being particularly cagey about her responses, knowing whatever she said would cause herself pain, but realising she had to earn the man's respect before he would talk to her. Now it seemed Eva had a starring role in her own movie.

She kept all that to herself though. She was going to need all her nerve for the conversation ahead. Eva rarely thought of her dad now. It was a part of her life that she'd put in a box and closed the lid on, sealing it down with thick tape that would take a while to budge. It was the reason she didn't want to see her brother as well. It would be too painful.

She thought for a moment about which parts of her own story would resonate with Alex, while not giving out too much detail, dredging up a past that she didn't want to discuss.

'My dad wasn't a very nice man,' she said. 'There were no family outings, no parties, no presents. For the most part, he would be in the pub.'

'Was he an alcoholic?'

'I expect so.'

'Did you love him?'

'As a child it's hard not to, isn't it?' Eva wanted to get Alex talking too. 'I thought he should love me, but treating my mum the way he did went against the grain. I wanted to love him, but he wasn't there enough.'

'Was he mean to you?'

'No.'

'But he changed everything for you on that day, didn't he?'

'Yes.' Eva was choked as memories flooded her mind. Visions of her father staggering in and taking his anger out on her mum. As a child in her bed at night, she'd squeeze her eyes tightly and cover her ears with her hands to drown out the sounds. Even now, the scent of cheap aftershave would make her shudder, taking her back to that time.

'So what happened?' Alex asked.

'I-I don't want to talk about it.'

'You haven't got any choice about that. If you don't tell me, then you won't eat.'

Eva wanted to say she would never mention her father if it weren't for getting out of this shithole in one piece. She wanted to say that it was inhumane to treat her like this.

Yet already she was thinking on her feet. She assumed this whole episode was something to do with how Alex had been treated in the past. She recalled the case only too well. The twins had been locked in a room for days on end. Perhaps this was Alex's way of coping with it. Reliving it but on her own terms.

Of course, Eva was here to tell Alex's story. Yet she would have done that anyway if she'd got in touch. For some reason, Alex wanted everyone to know who she was, and yet she would most probably be sent to prison if people found out.

Eva wanted to know about the other women too; the journalist in her needed to finish the story.

'Do you remember any good times with him?' Alex went on.

Eva shook her head, then realised she couldn't be seen through the wall. 'Not really. My life before it happened is a bit of a blur.'

'So is mine. That's something we have in common, pushing away a painful past.'

'What do you mean?' Eva wished she'd open up too.

'Until Ian turned up, life was okay. I had a really pleasant childhood before my dad died. He was a wonderful man. He'd take me and Jude for long walks, and for trips out with Mum too. Anyway, do continue.'

'I recall…' Eva halted.

'Are you pausing because you're trying not to think of something to talk about, or because you can't actually summon up anything?'

'The memories I have are vague. A trip to a sweetshop on a Sunday. My dad would give me all the spare change in his pockets and I could choose what I wanted.'

'Aww, that's nice. What else?'

Eva ran a hand through her hair, then grimaced, aghast at its lank, greasy state. The dirt underneath the gel coating on her nails. The smell emanating from her after four days in the cellar.

Think, think – what could she say? And then a memory flashed up.

'I had a friend called Tracy. Her family lived over a pub, and I'd often go there with my dad and he'd send me upstairs so he could drink in the bar. It was a huge flat with lots of rooms, and we used to play hide and seek for hours.' She found herself smiling, thinking back to an innocent time in her life, before everything changed. 'I loved it there.'

'That's not a happy memory about your dad,' Alex retorted. 'That's somewhere you wanted to be instead of being with him.'

'Yes, I suppose you're right. But he wasn't a nice man and I can't really recollect any times I was pleased to see him.'

'Did you ever go on holiday as a kid?'

'Not that I can recall.'

'You can't remember anywhere you've been with your dad?'

'No.'

'You're lying.'

'I'm not.' Eva could tell Alex was losing patience. 'Why would I keep things from you? Look, I can make things up but that wouldn't be fair. I genuinely can't recall a time when we went on holiday. I don't think we did much as a family. I think that's why he left in the end.'

'How long was he away for?'

'We never saw him for a year. I was happier. It was much better when it was just us.'

'And when he came back?'

'He didn't.'

'What?'

'He just turned up one afternoon, drunk. There was a row and…' Eva squeezed shut her eyes as pools of red invaded them. That metallic smell hanging in the air. She knew Alex would be waiting for her to speak but she was unable to. She let out a sob.

'What did you see?'

'I can't talk about it.' Eva dragged herself over to the mattress and sat with her back to the wall. She could see the life she had beyond the small hole in the door and up the stairs. If only she was tiny enough to fit through it, she'd be out in a flash. She pulled her knees in tight to her chest and hugged them.

'Eva?'

She said nothing.

'Eva!'

Still she said nothing.

'Talk to me.'

'Tomorrow, please.'

'I want to know now.'

'Tomorrow.'

There was silence and Eva was determined not to break into it first. She heard a dramatic sigh.

'Okay, okay. Have it your way.'

Eva was in no mood to join in any further. She needed to regroup, ready for whatever Alex threw at her next. Think of things to say to make the game more interesting. She had been ill-prepared until it had just revealed itself to her. Now she had time to invent memories, to gain more empathy, get Alex to engage more. If it made the long days go faster, she was all for it. Alex would never know what was truth or lies, as Eva hadn't spoken about it to anyone. Alex would only know what she had read online, and that was from a long time ago now.

But then Alex played her trump card.

'You have a brother, don't you?'

Eva squeezed her eyes tightly shut. Alex had sure done her research.

'I want to know all about him too.'

Before she could respond, the hatch was closed and Eva was left sitting in despair from the instant dismissal. She let her tears fall now, hoping they would be a comfort to her.

She was all alone again.

But she didn't want to talk about Daniel, or her father. And she prayed Alex wouldn't want to talk about her mother, her sweet, beautiful and kind mum.

Alex held all the cards. There was no way Eva could do her own thing. She had to stay compliant, if only from the outside.

AUGUST 2019

CHAPTER THIRTY-SEVEN

Stephanie Harvey

Stephanie sat alone in the conservatory. She couldn't believe that the journalist had gone missing too. She'd been interviewed by Eva Farmer twice now, and both times she'd shown empathy and understanding. It seemed more than a news item to her, as if she wanted to find out who was behind the abductions not just for her job, but for them all. Like her own kind of justice, or closure.

When she'd been released, Stephanie had been shocked and had struggled to get anything across to Eva. She never thought she'd see her family again. Her husband, her sons, her sister and her parents.

Everyone assumed she remembered things, too, and that she didn't want to talk about them, but it wasn't like that. She couldn't recall being abducted, and she still didn't know how she got away afterwards.

She could recall clearly being in that room for days on end, with no one to talk to and hardly any food. It was as if she didn't exist for ten days, and yet she had no idea who would do that to her.

And then it had been all over. She still didn't know why, or who she'd been taken by, but she knew she'd be looking over her shoulder for the rest of her life.

Her mind flicked back to the night she was set free. She was found wandering down the high street, naked, dirty and dishevelled. Luckily, she was found by a couple. The man took off his coat and wrapped it around her shoulders while the woman rang the police.

It wasn't until later that she realised her hair had been cut. Her beautiful red curls that used to trail down her back had been hacked off by what looked like a child. She had red lipstick smeared over her mouth as if she'd run the back of her hand over it, and black eyes. But they weren't from the mascara. They were fresh bruises.

Of course, she'd told the police all she knew. She didn't know of anyone who would harm her in that way. She had lived a very sedentary life.

She remembered the press and media going wild. She wasn't allowed to go home for two days. Michael and the boys came to her and they stayed in a hotel under supervision. And when they did leave, there were so many journalists outside the house it was ridiculous.

And scores of stories and comments from the general public. Stephanie could see people looking at her, wondering if she was telling the truth. Online was even worse. There were comments galore.

How could she not know where she's been?

Surely she must have seen who it was.

Who would cut her hair and leave her naked? Sounds like a madman to me.

She can't be telling the truth. I think there's something wrong with her marriage.

But why would she be lying? And no one could say that about Eva either. She had been kind, compassionate and empathetic whenever she'd spoken to her. She'd kept her informed of when the features were running, if anyone had come forward to the newspaper with information.

One of the first questions Stephanie had been asked by the police was if she knew anyone who bore a grudge. But she couldn't think of a single person. She was a married, middle-aged, nondescript woman, with two children and a home that would be paid for next year. She went to the gym twice a week, didn't eat many carbs and had a group of friends who she wouldn't call close but who she did have fun with every now and then. She wasn't ashamed to say she was what some would call a little boring.

Her boys and her husband were what kept her going when she'd been locked in that room. She and Michael had been married for seventeen years; the twins, Jasper and Kit, were now seven. Each day of her captivity, she'd tried to visualise their faces, their voices, their traits and foibles to stay grounded, even when she was convinced she was going to die of starvation or lack of water, or be held captive for the rest of her life.

But the worst thing? She didn't know if it would happen again. Why was she released after ten days without a word? It just didn't make sense.

One thing was certain, it was right what she'd said to Eva earlier in the year. It had changed her life completely.

She was no longer carefree and happy. She would always be fearful and anxious.

She would never be the Stephanie Harvey she was before.

And now it seemed Eva was going to suffer the same fate.

19 JULY 2019

CHAPTER THIRTY-EIGHT

Alex and Milly

I thought it best to meet Milly in the pavilion café today. It's in the park, where we first met on the bench. I'm a bit jittery about Jillian Bradshaw being in the cellar. Even though Milly has been to my house when I have had the other women hidden downstairs, there is something more challenging about Jillian.

I often wonder if Milly ever sees anything dark in me. She doesn't have a clue that I am the 'man' the police are after, and I like that. I don't want anything to spoil our friendship. I don't expect Milly would be too pleased if she found out what I've been up to. Still, she's not in any danger with me.

I sit watching the door. She's only a few minutes late and I'm already disappointed by the idea that she won't show. I glance around the room as I sip at my cappuccino. There are several groups of teenagers dotted around. A woman with a tiny baby alongside her is reading on a Kindle as she drinks a pot of tea. She keeps peering inside the pram and smiling to herself, and then returning to her book.

I've never experienced that maternal pull women speak about. My biological clock doesn't have a battery, never mind started to tick. And who can blame me with my background? I can never bring a child into the world as I know it. I didn't even want a pet. I am perfectly fine by myself.

The door opens and Milly comes bustling in. Out of school uniform, she looks older than her fifteen years. Her blonde hair is loose today and she wears a denim skirt, striped T-shirt and flat sandals. She makes her way through to my table.

'Hi, sorry I'm late. Mum made me tidy my room and do some ironing before I could come out.' She rolls her eyes. 'I'll grab a milkshake.'

I don't have time to speak to her before she is off. That's what I love about teenagers. They are full of energy, always going from one drama to another. I suspect Milly still doesn't have many friends at school, but I'm so glad that everything has been sorted out with the bullying. Jaimie has a good chance to sort herself out too.

'How are you?' Milly asks when she is back with her drink. 'Oh, sorry, I didn't ask if you wanted anything.'

'I'm fine.' I wave away her apology. 'My week's been okay. How about yours?'

'Okay, I suppose. Did you finish last week's book? I'm dying to talk about it. I loved it!'

I pick up the paperback and nod. We discuss our likes and dislikes for the next ten minutes or so. When I look into the room again, most of it is empty. But there is a man sitting in the window on his own. He smiles at me as I catch his eye. It's one of interest, I can tell.

I smile back and drop my eyes. When I glance at him again, he's still looking my way. I'm about to smile again but the café door opens and a woman comes dashing in almost as quickly as Milly did. I can tell she's apologising for being late too. She sits next to him rather than across from him and gives him a kiss.

I glower at him. I detest men who give the impression they're free when they are nothing of the sort. A bit of sex would have cheered me up. Instead, he's left me feeling deflated. Fucking idiot.

Milly is saying something, but I haven't been listening. Quickly, I absorb myself back into the conversation.

'So what book shall we choose next then?' Milly says.

'How about you decide and text me the title?' I offer.

Milly nods. 'Cool.'

'I don't mind what you pick so long as it isn't too mushy. You know I like my fiction dark. Do you have any of Stephen King's?'

'I have *The Shining* and *Misery* in paperback. I've read them both but I can read them again.'

'Great! Which one?'

'Umm. *Misery*?'

'It's a deal.'

As we leave, I walk past the man's table, deliberately knocking into him as he's holding his cup to his mouth. The liquid flies across the table and into his lap.

'Oh, I'm so sorry,' I say. 'How clumsy of me.'

He stands up and throws me a filthy look as the woman hands him a few paper napkins.

'Let me get you another one,' I purr.

'It's fine,' he replies. 'There wasn't much left anyway.'

I glance down and then up before staring at him. 'What a pity we didn't get to share more than a smile while you were waiting for her to get here.'

I leave the café a little lighter than when I arrived. I can already hear the woman questioning him. Stupid idiot.

DAY 5

17 August 2019

CHAPTER THIRTY-NINE

Alex

I called the office this morning and faked illness, and then I sat watching TV for most of the day. Eva is still in the headlines. The police are no further forward, although they hint of an ongoing investigation looking into a certain lead. I wonder what that's all about, reassured they probably won't be talking about me. They couldn't possibly be. And in a few days it will all be pointless anyway.

I go over my conversation with Eva. It's like that story I'd heard about, the *Arabian Nights*, where the husband was going to murder his wife after she'd told him a story, but she was clever enough to end it on a cliffhanger each night so she was spared death. That's how Eva must be feeling now. I giggle.

But then just as quickly my thoughts darken. I hate how it's dredged up memories of that place: Winterdale Children's Home. It will forever be a blot on my landscape. An ink stain I will never be able to rid myself of.

At the home, I was corralled in for breakfast at half past seven. I'd be out of the door, heading for school, before eight a.m., desperate to get some time alone. Often I didn't make it to classes. I'd hang around the park, keeping out of everyone's way. I'd do anything not to be with others.

The home was a desperate place. I yearned for a family who would look after me, love me as their own, but there was never one. I'd been fielded out several times before eventually everyone gave up on me. It wasn't my fault I couldn't settle. Had they taken time to find out why, maybe none of this would have happened.

I hope Eva got all that down, is writing it all out in full for me now. I will look over it this evening, see if she's doing a good job or not. She'd better show me in a good light, that's all I have to say on the matter.

Half an hour has passed, and I'm still trying to block out memories as they come rushing back to me. I had no idea the experience would leave me so drained. It isn't just listening to Eva talking about her childhood that's upsetting. It's knowing that I'll have to tell her what happened to Jude. I rarely have a day when I don't think of him, even after all these years.

No one understands what it's like to lose a twin, especially after what we'd been through together. My brother had always looked out for me until that fateful day. And what made it worse was he'd taken the blame for something he hadn't done.

A part of me had died that day too. The connection that only twins could have. We had been a team. I will never forget how his life was cut short and he was taken away from me.

I often wonder what he would have been like if he was still alive. Would he have a wife, or a child by now? Would I be with someone, married too? Happy, perhaps, instead of living this soul-destroying life?

I have no idea of knowing and I don't feel that is fair. Do you?

CHAPTER FORTY

Eva

Eva had been crying for over an hour, her body needing the release because of the pain she'd dredged up that morning. She didn't talk about her past for good reason. She hated what it had done to her as a child.

It had seemed strange having a conversation through a wall at first, but after a while it was as if it wasn't there at all. How she wished that were true, that she could run up those steps and out of captivity. Eva was so scared right now. Fearful of being left alone, terrified of what was going to happen to her, worried that she would never see Nick or the outside of this room ever again.

She'd tried to think happy thoughts but it had only worked for so long. She yearned for it to be night again when she could hide in the shadows of the dark. Close her eyes tightly and pretend this had never happened as she drifted off to medication-induced sleep. Wake up to this all being a dream. A nightmare, but one she could escape from. That any minute now she'd be sitting up to see Nick beside her, waiting to comfort her. He would take her in his arms and she would be safe by his side, drifting gently back to sleep and leaving all this behind.

She retched at the smell of her own body odour. She couldn't stand the thought that she hadn't washed in five days.

How had it come to this? What had she done to deserve it? While she had fight left in her, she was going to find out. But for now, she had to keep picturing herself at home with Nick. He would keep her going through the silent days and the dark nights.

She thought of what they were supposed to have been doing that weekend for his mother's birthday. They were due to have lunch with Nick's parents, at their local pub. The Valley Arms was a beautiful establishment, blending the old with the new. They often sat in the large conservatory overlooking fields, a reservoir in the distance. The doors would be open at this time of year, a slight breeze blowing through, and they'd be chatting, drinking and sharing good food and anecdotes. They'd drive home after saying their goodbyes, even then looking forward to the next visit.

Eva liked her in-laws and really hoped that one day she would get to say happy birthday to Margaret. Although she'd got on well with her aunt and uncle, her in-laws were like the parents she'd never had. She'd lost a delightful mother, taken from her so cruelly at such a young age. So finding Nick's mum to be such a loving person had been good for her. Margaret was wonderful. On her last birthday, she had insisted on buying Eva flowers and chocolates too.

And soon she might possibly get the chance to be a mother herself. After all the time they'd been trying, it was only now she got caught. She hoped she'd be there to tell Nick the good news. To see him take her in his arms and cry tears of happiness with her.

She longed to hold her own child, to press it to her breast and nourish it. To see it grow and watch it develop. Her and Nick's child.

That was her reason for getting out of here. No matter how hard it became, she would think of nothing else. Over and over and over.

AUGUST 2019

CHAPTER FORTY-ONE

Nick Farmer

Nick took a quick shower. He'd had a terrible day, the results of something he'd expected to work in his favour turning out not to do so.

Having been removed from the abduction case, along with Jill's husband, for personal reasons, he was at a loose end. Neither of them was in the office right now. Instead they met up, like two lost children waiting for their mums to come and collect them.

Under the water, he let his tears fall, wondering how Eva was, where she was. What she would be doing. He hoped she wouldn't be suffering too much mental and physical trauma. He'd be lost without her if she didn't return soon.

He *was* lost without her. He just wanted her home.

Everyone was tiptoeing around him and Steve. But they weren't being helpless. They were still involved in some of the strategic work going on to find their partners. They were also supporting each other, trying to hold their heads high, telling themselves Jill and Eva were both still alive. Because the alternative didn't bear thinking about.

Two days ago, the team thought they'd had a lead. They'd found a connection: a man named Ed Barker. He was known to all the women, but after being picked up and interviewed for some time, they had nothing on him. His alibis stood up; he wasn't their man. On every occasion a woman had gone missing, he'd been at work, mainly out of the city, so they'd had to let him go.

During most cases, they relied on the public for general information. A phone call from a neighbour when someone was acting suspiciously; a message from a relative who was worried about a son. Gossip around an estate if you spent enough time collecting it could lead to dividends. That was what his job largely entailed: listening to people, and wheedling out information.

But they couldn't do that this time. There was nothing to go on. And it was so hard to contemplate. It stung that even though he'd been taken off the case, he couldn't help anyway. Eva had no enemies. She was a journalist with a conscience. She wasn't one of the doorstop brigade who barged into peoples' lives without a second thought to their welfare.

In the bedroom, he pulled back the duvet and got into bed, wondering where Eva was, if she was sleeping. Had she even got a bed to sleep in? He remembered the other women saying they'd slept on a dirty mattress in what looked like a cellar.

Nick reached for Eva's pillow, drawing it into his chest and wrapping his arms around it. Like he'd done every night since she'd gone missing, he sniffed in the scent of her, still on the sheets, as more tears dropped onto his own pillow. Why did this have to happen after Jill Bradshaw hadn't come home?

The worst was the not knowing how Eva was doing. The agony of missing her, worrying about her. Not having her close. His mind would often go blank and he'd stare ahead, as if by some miracle she would appear at the door and climb into bed with him. His body ached for her at the mere thought.

Nick recalled the first time he'd met her. His DCI had been retiring and they were all in the pub. Eva's friends were celebrating a birthday. He'd caught her eye and she'd smiled at him.

When one of the officers he worked with had gone to speak to Eva, he'd sidled over and joined in. Before long, they'd been the only two people sitting at the table and had spent the rest of the evening getting to know each other.

Within two weeks of dating, he'd known he would marry her. It was a cliché but they were good together. Their jobs probably kept their relationship alive rather than allowing them to get into a rut. It made them appreciate the precious time they spent together around shift work. And between the two of them there was always something to talk about.

Eva shared his love of *Transformers*. Across a planned weekend, they'd sit for hours bingeing the franchise. They'd buy in popcorn and beer and order in takeaways and slob out on the settee. It was their thing. She'd even bought him a lamp for the bedroom in the shape of Optimus Prime.

He stared at it now, wishing he had super powers to reach out into Eva's mind and see where she was. Rescue her and bring her home.

He reached for his phone but there were no new messages, squeezed his eyes tight as tears formed again. The only consolation was they were closing in on the abductor.

He prayed Eva and Jill were safe until they found them.

DAY 6

18 August 2019

CHAPTER FORTY-TWO

Alex

I have no work this morning so I cook myself an English breakfast. While the bacon is sizzling away, I take Eva her tea and toast and leave her to it. I bet she can smell my food. I laugh, hoping it makes her hungry.

A few minutes later, I go downstairs again. Eva pushes through the empty tray, and I sit down behind the door.

'Let's talk about Maxine Stallington, woman number two,' I say to her. 'She was quite a sweet old soul, if truth be known. But she failed me, as she didn't do what she was supposed to do.'

'In what way?'

'She was my social worker. She was allocated to me when I was taken into care. Up to the date of the trial, I was fostered with this lovely family. When my mum and Ian were jailed, and there were no other relatives to look after me, Maxine was put in charge of finding me a more permanent place to stay. I ended up in Winterdale, a home for kids. She took me from a place where I was happy and put me somewhere I hated.

'After a while I was sent to live with another family. They wanted to adopt me but they were hideous to me. At first, I rebelled, but then I realised it was easier to be quiet about things, blend in to the background so I was no trouble to anyone. Then once I had their trust, I could get away with things, blame them on other people. But I was sent back to the children's home. I was a schemer then too – a planner. And boy did I plan my revenge and what I would do once I was old enough.'

I find myself unable to stop talking once I start. It's as if a valve has been released.

'Maxine had to write a welfare report to say where she thought I would be best placed. She mentioned the foster home I was in could never be a place for me to settle permanently and had only been a temporary measure. She said I needed a stable placement, with people who could give me the attention I deserved.'

'That sounds like someone who cared about you,' Eva said.

'She didn't. She wanted to close my case and move on to the next reprobate. And she never checked up to see I was okay. Because I wasn't. It was one of the most traumatic times in my life. I had seen my brother die and been removed from my family home. My mum was in prison, and I was taken to a place I wasn't familiar with, to live with people who didn't know me.

'My brother was dead because of Maxine. She should have checked up on us more when Jude was alive. I knew, even back then, that one day I would make her pay. You see, I'll never forget that home. Every beating I took off the older kids. Every person who came into my room at night-time and shouldn't have.

'I saw her photo in the newspaper. She may be old and grey now, but I remember her very differently. When I was ten, she had dark hair. She wore high heels. Bright clothes and lipstick too. She must have been about fifty at the time. I looked up to her and yet she didn't do what's best for me. She did what she had to, I suppose, but I wanted someone to fight for me. I wanted someone who would look out for me, visit me regularly and see how I was doing. I was a child! No one should be left alone like that.

'Maxine said she'd find someone special to look after me. She didn't do a good job of that, did she? My foster parents were appalling. Oh, they didn't harm me in any way. I wasn't abused physically or sexually, thankfully. But mentally? They didn't want me there. They wanted the money that came with looking after me. I went into myself, stayed out of their way. Never made a noise, hardly ever came out of my room.'

'Were you fostered more than once?' Eva asks.

'Yes, lots of times. I lost count. No one really liked me.'

'I'm sure that's not true.'

I ignore her and continue, 'When Maxine came to see me at the home, she asked if everything was all right. Of course, I said it was fine. But she should have known better, been able to see that I was lying. That I was dying inside from the lack of love and affection I craved.

'I stayed at that home for a while before being fostered out again, and again, and again. Each time I was sent back because I was emotionally damaged. Well, yes, can you imagine what seeing your brother murdered does to a child? How it messed with my head? Maxine couldn't. And she should have. It was her job to look after me and she failed.'

'I'm sorry to hear you feel that way, Alex,' Eva replied.

'Oh, enough about me. I'm fine. It was years ago.' A slight pause. 'What's your favourite flower?'

'What?'

'Small talk, Eva. Humour me.'

'I suppose it would be lilies.'

'Mine would be roses, although I don't get them too often.' I laugh. 'Anyway, I've chatted for way too long. It's your turn now. Tell me about the night your dad killed your mum.'

CHAPTER FORTY-THREE

Eva

The sharp contrast in how upset Alex had been and then how she changed in an instant unnerved Eva. It was as if Alex could switch her emotions off with the flick of a switch. One minute she was chatty and upbeat, the next she was angry, wanting to know all about Eva instead. Alex was clearly playing mind games, but Eva didn't want to join in. She felt so helpless, being left in the dark.

She thought back to meeting Maxine Stallington's daughter, when her mother had been kidnapped.

'I've been following how you've been reporting about Mum,' Sandra told her over a coffee as they sat at the kitchen table. 'Some journalists have been ruthless, telling lies about her. Saying she's just gone off and not telling anyone where she is. But I know her better than that. She's missing.'

Tears trickled down her face and she wiped at them furiously.

Eva reached across and placed a hand on her arm. 'I'm so sorry you're having to go through this. You say you haven't heard anything for over a week now?'

Sandra shook her head. 'I can't sleep. I can't leave her house either. My husband is looking after our children. I just want to be here in case she turns up again.' She looked at Eva. 'She will turn up again, I'm certain.'

'Let's hope so.' Eva got out her notepad and sat down. 'Do you mind if I take some notes?'

'Not at all, although I can't tell you anything else that I haven't told the police.'

'I don't want to know any more than how she was as a mother to you all. I want to tell Maxine's story, nothing to do with her going missing. Would you help me do that? I promise not to print anything you don't want me to. I'm not someone who wants to cause distress while selling a few more papers. I know journalists get a bad name because, well, a lot of them are ruthless. But I'm not one for telling tales. I like to get to the heart of the story.'

Sandra had visibly relaxed. She had gained her trust. That was what she had to do to Alex. She had to keep her onside too.

'Come on. It's your turn!'

Alex's sharp shout made Eva jump, bringing her back to reality. It was time to play the game, no matter how damaging it would be for her own mental health.

'I was twelve when it happened,' Eva started. 'My mum had got divorced from my dad and I hadn't seen him since then. It had been the best year of my life. Without the threat of him coming home drunk, getting angry with my mum and often hitting her, it was a lovely time. But then, one day...'

Eva closed her eyes as the memories came back.

'What did you see?' Alex encouraged her after Eva had been quiet for a few seconds.

'My mum was lying on the floor, blood all over her. Her head was turned my way and she stared at me with empty eyes.' Eva would never forget that look for as long as she lived. 'My dad was sitting on the settee with his head in his hands. The knife was at his feet. When he saw me, he looked up for a moment and said he was sorry, over and over.'

'What did you do?'

'I froze. I didn't know whether I should go to my mum or leave the room and dial 999. I was worried my dad might pick up the knife again. I was scared to move. In the end, I burst into tears and dropped to the floor to see for myself what I already knew. I shook my mum's shoulder, trying to get her to wake up. But she didn't move.'

Eva held back a sob as memories of her screaming at her dad came back to her. 'What have you done! What have you done!' She recalled him coming out of his trance and standing up quickly. He'd held out his hand, stepping towards her. Eva had thought he was going to attack her next, so she'd cowered.

'I wish I could have stuck a knife in Ian. Jude would still be alive now,' Alex said. 'He was so cruel. What happened to your dad?'

'He turned the knife on himself.'

'Aren't you angry that he took his own life, rather than getting justice for your mum?'

'Back then I would have been too upset. My dad murdered my mum, and I hated him but he was dead. You must know how that feels.'

'I do. So what happened then?'

'The ambulance and the police came. Afterwards, I was taken to my aunt's home with my brother.'

Eva wiped away her tears. Her aunt and uncle had been saints. They'd had two teenagers forced upon them and yet they'd never complained. It took a long time for Eva to accept that her mum was gone forever, but they helped her through it.

Telling her story had drained her. She might be giving Alex the upper hand by showing her own emotions too, but it had consequences.

Yet something was telling Eva to keep going, build up that rapport by talking and listening, even though it was hard going. It brought back many memories she'd chosen to bury deep. Resurrecting them meant she had ample time to think about them again. And her brother, Daniel, too.

Because Eva hadn't told Alex the truth about what really happened the day her mum was murdered.

CHAPTER FORTY-FOUR

Alex

I feel sorry for Eva but I am tired of listening to her. She's not here to rid herself of all her demons. She's here to help me now. Yet I can't help but give her a moment to compose herself as I can hear her sniffling.

'Don't cry, Eva,' I tell her. 'Not until you've heard my story anyway.' I wait for her to settle before beginning. 'My dad was a wonderful man. I have lots of memories of him, and us as a family. He used to take us to the seaside quite a lot. His parents ran a caravan park by the sea. We'd go down there most weekends. Me and Jude would be off on the beach, or playing on the slot machines.' I laugh. 'The year before he died, there were wild rabbits underneath the vans and we'd stand for hours waiting to pounce on one and cover it with a cardboard box. We were convinced we were going to catch one for a pet. We never did. Did you get on with your brother, Eva?'

'He's four years older than me but yes, I suppose I did.'

'And now?'

'I haven't seen him for a while.'

'Why not?'

'He works away.'

'I often wonder what my life would have been like if Jude hadn't died. Do you ever think the same?'

'Yes, but I wasn't close to my brother. Not like you and Jude.'

'When we were about four, me and Jude used to climb on Dad's shoulders, one of us sitting on each. He'd race around the room with us, being careful not to bump our heads on the ceiling and bobbing down through doorways. We would laugh so much and hold hands to steady ourselves.'

'Were your mum and dad happy before he died?'

'Yes, until I was eight, I had a normal life.'

'I bet that was nice.'

'It was. We didn't have much but we were well looked after. There were many happy times. And then, it all stopped when he died.'

'How did it happen?'

'Cancer. One minute he was okay and the next he'd collapsed with a headache. Apparently he had a tumour so large they couldn't operate, and he was dead five weeks later.'

'I'm sorry to hear that. It must have been a shock.'

'It was.' I pause for a moment, swallowing hard before my grief gives me away. 'We were all devastated. That was when everything went wrong.'

'Because you were without him?'

'No, because Mum met *him* a year later and he moved in. Ian didn't like us kids. Looking back, I reckon he needed somewhere to stay and Mum was afraid to say no. We were scared of him but we couldn't do anything about it. We were glad when we were at school and away from him. Which is why he chose the long summer holiday to do what he did.'

I stand up quickly. I can feel my temper rising. I've had enough for one day. Without another word, I fasten the hatch and race upstairs. I need a drink to calm my nerves. Before I do something I regret.

Because it's talking to Eva that is dredging up the past, making my feelings come to the top again. And I don't like that. I don't like that at all.

AUGUST 2019

CHAPTER FORTY-FIVE

Maxine Stallington

Maxine sat on the settee, the TV news on. Images of Eva Farmer were popping up every few minutes, and she assumed lots of people would be glued to it.

Eva Farmer was a lovely woman and she didn't deserve what had happened to her, not for doing her job. Like everyone, Maxine was hoping Eva would be set free after ten days, especially since the fourth woman hadn't come home as she and the others had.

'Are you okay, Mum?' Her daughter, Sandra, came into the room with two mugs of tea. She put them on the coffee table and sat down next to her.

'Oh, I'm fine, love,' Maxine replied. 'I'm just worried about Eva Farmer.'

'I hate to see you so distressed. Watching this must bring it all back to you.'

Maxine nodded, unable to put her thoughts into words. It had been hard being locked in that room, knowing that Stephanie Harvey had been in there for ten days previously. At the time, Maxine hadn't thought she'd survive long enough to be set free. She wasn't even sure she would be set free at all.

The silence had been draining. She could hear the sound of her own breathing all the time. Occasionally, she'd catch a bit of music, or a few footsteps above her.

She'd shouted out at first, almost losing her voice with the effort. But after waking up bruised and beaten, she hadn't tried that again. Her captive was a coward, always drugging her before coming into the room to assault her. After that she had been silent for the rest of the ordeal, trying to ignore the mental and physical need for contact, the thought she was deteriorating so quickly.

'Do you want to talk about anything?'

Maxine shook her head and reached for her daughter's hand. 'It doesn't help at all.'

She wished she could switch her thoughts off, but since the journalist had gone missing, she'd been in a permanent state of trepidation. The newsreader on the TV was homing in on Eva's husband. Maxine could see the stress in his features. He looked as if he hadn't slept since she'd gone missing. At least her husband hadn't been put through what he must be going through right now.

She glanced around the room. Coming back hadn't been as easy as she'd imagined. All the time she'd been in that cellar, she'd thought of nothing else. Before her abduction, she used to be fine living by herself. It had only been six months since Barry had died – they were together for nearly forty years – and she'd still felt his presence around the house.

But now? She didn't feel him with her any more. She feared he'd disowned her after what happened. It was silly, she knew, and she would never tell any of her family that. But it was the one thing she couldn't cope with.

She remembered telling Eva Farmer how she would have killed herself during her imprisonment, but she hadn't been able to find anything to do it with. Now, she looked around her home and saw lots of things she could use. But she had made a promise to herself, and to Barry, when she was in that room. If she made it out, she would stick around to see who it was who had kidnapped her. Because she wanted to know why, needed to know why. To understand. Why her?

Previously, the police had asked her lots of questions. Did she see who it was? Did she know where she was held? But she couldn't tell them anything. All she could say was that her recollection was the same as Stephanie Harvey's. It seemed as if they had been kept in the same room, held by the same man.

Let go by the same man. An insane man, no doubt.

DAY 6

18 August 2019

CHAPTER FORTY-SIX

Alex

As soon as I get back into the kitchen, I open the fridge and take out most of its contents, spreading it on the table. Butter, cheese, ham, yoghurts, a milkshake. I grab the bread that's open, a jar of peanut butter, jam and a packet of crackers. And then there is the cake that's half eaten.

I get a plate and sit down for my feast. I make a jam buttie to start, slicing cheese and adding it to crackers as I eat. Then I have toast and peanut butter, washed down with milkshake.

I can't get it in my mouth quick enough. Each bite of food is like a diversion from thinking about everything I've said to Eva. All these chats with her are raking up memories that I don't want in my life again.

I close my eyes and Jude invades my thoughts. We're playing sharks and custard. There isn't much we can jump on, as we only have the two beds and our pillows and blankets. But we've been leaping about for ages and it's great fun. But then Ian comes into the room and, as I am nearest to the door, slaps me so hard my ear rings for days. When he's gone an arm comes around my shoulder as my brother cuddles up to me.

I wish he could do that so much right now that I virtually feel his presence beside me.

Almost telepathically, a message comes in from Milly. It's the weekend and she's at a loose end, asking if I want to meet for coffee. I message back, not bothering to wipe the butter from my fingers, saying I'm busy. Well, I am, aren't I? I have to keep Eva entertained. She is my main priority right now.

Although it breaks my heart to turn Milly down. She has been good for me and I won't see her again after next week. So I arrange for her to come to tea in the week. It will be her last time, but she won't know that. I'll make it special for her. Because once the story breaks in the news, she's not going to think much of me.

I wonder if she will be totally shocked or if she has sensed a bad vibe from me every now and then. For the most part, I think I've kept my temper under control when I've been with her. It's because she's so innocent, so sweet, and she makes me laugh. She's been like a breath of fresh air since the Jaimie business was sorted out too. And she has other friends now. She wouldn't have got those without me.

I've eaten so much my stomach is fit to burst, but still I continue, moving on to the two slices of cake and half a packet of biscuits. They are the only things I have left in the house now. I'll have to nip to the local shop tomorrow.

Finally, I feel the need to purge it all, get rid of the garbage inside of me along with the crap I've just eaten. In the bathroom, I force the food out of me. My chest and throat are sore by the time I've finished, my hair wet with sweat. The weather is stifling outside, even late into the evening, and the bathroom is a tiny room with one small window.

I lie on the tiles to get cool, and close my eyes. But that brings up images of Jude. My beautiful brother. My lost soul.

The worst thing about being in care was that no one really acknowledged I had lost him. Everyone wanted to know how I was coping, because so much had happened to me, but they didn't address how much I was grieving for my brother.

I tried to kill myself a few times, but they were cries for help, not real attempts. I wanted someone to tell me why I survived and Jude didn't. What was so special about me that I was spared? Why wasn't it me who died? Jude was much stronger than me.

Eventually I sit up, wash away the sick around my mouth and from my hands and start to feel a tad more normal.

It is hard to keep up a front: too hard, at times. But I am not a victim any more. I've let that happen for far too long. I might seem weak but, actually, I'm quite strong. And I will have my revenge completely soon.

CHAPTER FORTY-SEVEN

Eva

Eva tried to sleep, but there was so much going round inside her head that even with the medication she found it hard to switch off. She couldn't understand why the women who had been abducted hadn't been linked to Alex, if they had been so nasty to her. It was pretty obvious the police hadn't found anything, so why not? Was it because Alex was lying? Making it up, to be more colourful than it was?

Of course, Alex needed help but Eva was confused. Why would Alex think that Maxine Stallington had done nothing for her? How could she then drug and kidnap a woman of her age? Beat her like a dog, starve her and treat her so cruelly? Was it so she would know how Alex had suffered as a child? But that was before she'd been taken into care.

And why would Alex want everyone to know about her story by committing crimes of her own? It could mean she'd go to prison. Or was she intent on ending her life instead, once she'd told her story?

Which left the question – what would Alex do with Eva? Would she leave her down there to starve to death, to rot all alone? Or would she let her go, so that she could pass on the story?

Either way it didn't bear thinking about.

But Eva had to. She had to keep doing her job, empathising with Alex to make her open up. She wanted this story to be sensational if she was released after ten days. She needed to get something from this ordeal, for what Alex had put her through. It would take her mind away from the reality of the situation, that she might not survive to tell it to anyone else.

She pressed the heel of her hands into her eyes to stop tears from forming. She was so tired, so dirty, so stressed that she didn't want to think of dying today. Last night, she had decided to win Alex over. She'd thought about what Nick would do in the same position. After first wanting to punch someone's lights out and break everything he could while trying to escape, he would befriend his abductor. So she had to use her own backstory more, see if she could connect by sharing her pain.

It was worth a shot to build up a connection, maybe keep the two-way conversation going between them. Perhaps then Alex wouldn't harm her. She didn't want to think about what had happened to Jill. For all she knew, she could be locked in another room, unable to hear her.

Still, there were some things that she couldn't talk about. She hadn't wanted to voice what she'd gone through as a child. Yes, she needed to gain empathy with Alex, but she also had to protect her own state of well-being, plus not give Alex too many advantages.

She hadn't been telling the truth about her dad. Her father hadn't been kind to her at all. She'd lived her life in fear, being scared to make a noise. Her mum had tried to leave with her and Daniel several times, but he'd always found her, begged her to come back to him. She realised now, for the sake of her and her brother while they were all stuck in one room, her mum had done the best she could. Eventually her dad had gone of his own accord and things had been great for quite some time. Until he'd come back that day.

An image so powerful it made her gasp came into her mind. She could still recall sitting by the side of her mum's body, willing her to open her eyes. The soft sobs of her dad sitting behind her. The sheer terror of realising this was real, that her life was changed forever.

Her mum, her beautiful mum. Who had helped her to do her hair every day, arranging it in the French plait she'd loved.

Who bought her everything she could and worked long hours to provide for her and her brother.

Who had been there for her when she was ill, when she'd run to her after school with a drawing she was proud of, or a test that she'd passed.

She'd always been there for her.

And in the blink of an eye she was gone.

And then Eva had a thought. Might she be able to get Alex talking about what happened to her and Jude if she spoke more about Daniel? There could be some information to use. She'd hate to relive things about that too, but she had to barter memories to get through this, to at least have a bit of nourishment to help the baby. So she wouldn't be starved of food and water, even the little she was being given.

She had three more nights to go. Three nights nearer to going home. To Nick, to her friends and family, to tell them the news about her baby.

She could do this. She would do this. For herself, for Nick and for baby Farmer.

DAY 7

19 August 2019

CHAPTER FORTY-EIGHT

Eva

Eva woke to another day where her stomach was in knots. Not only because of the pregnancy but because of the situation.

A whole week had passed. She might have less time to suffer than she had already gone through, but even that didn't make anything feel any better.

Regardless of the sedative in her drink, she'd had nightmares all night. Mentally she was drained. Trying to keep a positive spin on everything to help herself through was getting beyond her. And after talking about her dad yesterday and hearing Alex's story about hers, Eva was exhausted. Despite her thoughts last night about opening up more, it wasn't uncommon for them to change over a period of hours. She wasn't sure what to do for the best.

Alex had been quiet when she'd brought down her sandwich and drink last night. Eva had tried to talk to her, but she'd been ignored. So she was glad to hear her arrive outside her door this morning. Her breakfast was pushed through, and Eva dived on it immediately.

'It's Alison Green's time,' Alex said a few moments later. 'Are you ready with your notebook?'

'Yes.'

It seemed ridiculous to think that Alex was a metre away from Eva, and yet she couldn't see her. To listen to what Alex had to say, she sat with her back to the wall, as near to the door as possible. Who knew if Alex was sitting behind her, the wall the only thing between them?

'Alison was my foster parent,' Alex said. 'She was nice to me in front of social services. But when I was on my own, she was no better than that bastard Ian. She locked me in my room, like he had. How monstrous do you think that was after what he'd done?'

Eva held in a sigh. It didn't seem anything like Alison Green would do. It felt like something Alex was fabricating again. But she wrote it out, just as she'd been told.

'It must have been terrible to lose not only your brother, but your twin,' she encouraged. 'I don't know how you got over that.'

'I didn't. I became a different person, cut off from the "before" me. The "after" me isn't much better at living though.' She sniggered. 'The "older" me wants everyone to know that none of this is my fault.'

'I don't think anyone would blame you.'

'Really? I saw what the papers wrote. Reporters had their doubts about me, though I wasn't involved. They printed things about me anyway. They called me horrid names, crucified my reputation, even as a child. And then I had one man hound me when he found out who I was. That's why I changed my name. I never want to be that child again, especially without my brother by my side.'

Eva couldn't recall seeing anything like that in the press, although it was thirteen years ago. Perhaps there had been a rogue reporter who had said something and it had rightly gone ignored.

'I'm sorry we made you feel like that.'

'*You* didn't! You took a positive spin on my story and made me out to be a superhero. But I was ten years old. What was I supposed to believe?'

'That must have been hard to go through.'

'Of course it was, dur! But I was alive. And until I spoke to her, I wanted to die.'

Eva was so busy writing everything down that she'd lost Alex's chain of thought. But then she paused.

'Sorry, who?'

'My mother. I went to see her, once, in prison. She smiled at me, waving as I walked to her in the visiting room. When I sat down across from her, I could tell she thought I'd forgiven her because I'd turned up. All I wanted to do was spit in her face.' She laughed. 'And do you know? I did just that before I left. I spoke to her, told her how I was, told her how she made me feel. Explained in great detail how much I hated her, how much she had ruined my life. And when tears had poured down her face for long enough, I leaned over and I spat. Right in her face.' Alex laughed again. 'She wasn't even surprised. She just sat there with my saliva creeping down her cheek as I stood up. I told her I wouldn't be visiting again and that I hoped she'd rot in hell.'

Eva had stayed quiet, shocked, while she listened. It was as if Alex had been taken over, ranting away. As if something inside her had been released now she was telling her story. Maybe this would benefit her in the long-term. She desperately needed help. It seemed she couldn't distinguish the lies from the truth.

It was strange to hear Alex had suffered so much that she didn't recognise what was real and what she had made up. Eva didn't have sympathy after what she'd done to her and the other women, or what she was capable of doing. But she wasn't going to show that to Alex. She prayed Alex wouldn't start blaming her, though, when her story was finished and she read it back in full.

For now, there was nothing she could do but get the words down and hope to get out of there. Keep her thoughts to herself so Alex didn't see her as a threat. If that's what it took, she would stay calm, be the friend Alex seemed to need.

She looked around the cellar. One day she would be free of this… this disgusting hovel she was sleeping in, the nauseating scent of her own body and someone else's clothes she'd been wearing for the past week.

'Back to Alison Green!'

Alex interrupted Eva's thoughts, and she got ready to write again.

'I read the article in the *Stoke News* where she made out she was all sweet and innocent. She clearly had no idea what she and her family put me through. How dare she say she didn't remember me? I was with her for five months, straight after Jude died.'

Eva cast her mind back to one of their earlier conversations. Hadn't Alex said she was happy at the foster home until Maxine Stallington told her she'd have to go to the children's home?

'When I arrived at her house, I was shown to my bedroom. Her daughters were in another room and they ignored me completely. They made my life hell – so much so I thought at first I would abduct one of them instead of Alison. But then I realised it was her parenting skills – or lack of them – that had made them how they were. It was her fault they were such bitches.

'She made me try and fit in, no matter what. When I wanted to be on my own, she'd make me join in with "family stuff". How cruel was that after I was grieving for my brother? Jude was a part of my life I wasn't willing to leave behind, and she just wanted me to wipe my hands of him.'

'Do you think Alison was trying to involve you in her family, rather than make you forget your own?'

'No, I don't. Have you any idea how I felt trying not to think about Jude? The day he died, I couldn't protect him. I still remember the last time I was with him. How we held hands in the cold, huddled up together in a room the size of the one she gave me as a bedroom. I tried to keep him warm, to stop him soiling his clothes with vomit because I knew they wouldn't be washed, that we wouldn't be let out to wash ourselves. Jude meant the world to me, and Alison didn't want me to think about him.'

'I'm so sorry you had no one to speak to.' Eva wanted to keep Alex talking about Jude. 'Do you—'

'So now I've explained to you about three of the women,' Alex butted in. 'I wonder if the police are fitting together the clues I've left. Is your precious Nick cottoning on to who I am yet? I hope they don't find me before I finish my plan. I'm really enjoying this storytelling lark.'

At the mention of Nick, Eva crumpled. She shoved a fist into her mouth to stop from crying out, hoping to keep her pain from Alex. If Alex knew it was getting to her this much, she was sure to use it to her advantage. And to Eva's disadvantage. She couldn't allow that to happen.

'Do you want to tell me about Jude?' she asked, hoping to keep Alex talking. 'I'd love to hear more about him.'

CHAPTER FORTY-NINE

Alex

Sometimes I long to speak to Eva face to face. It would be much better to talk to her that way, but it isn't possible. I don't trust her. So instead, I sit outside the cellar, with my back to the wall, trying to picture her behind me.

'I speak to Jude all the time,' I say. 'I know he's still with me. And before you go thinking that I'm weird, don't bother. He isn't in my head. I see him in my mind as the little boy he was, but I don't hear voices, except my own. I feel him close to me whenever I'm lost. But ultimately I am the one who's making the decisions.

'The feeling of loss can get to me at any time. I can hear a song on the radio and it takes me back as quick as this.' I snap my fingers. 'I'll recall the good times. But then that brings back the bad memories too.

'I missed out on so many things with Jude. The weddings we should have had. The children. The dogs and cats we said we'd have as pets as soon as we were allowed. Christmas, birthdays – everything we would have done together. And I don't even have a picture of him.'

'It must have been terrible not to be able to help him,' Eva says. 'I'll never forget trying to wake my mum, but knowing she was dead. There was so much blood. No one could have survived that.'

'I knew Jude was dying, and I tried to get help but my mum didn't come. I was so weak through having hardly any food. He slipped away, and yet I fell asleep. The guilt was overwhelming: that it had been him who'd died and not me. There was anger that he'd been taken away so cruelly, and the fear of the unknown. What was going to happen to me now that he was gone? Now that my mum and him were in prison because of what they had done.

'I've been lonely all my life without Jude. You'll never understand unless you're a twin. When we were together, nothing mattered except the two of us. We got through everything thrown at us. He looked out for me; I looked out for him. It was the way it was. Were you like that with your brother, Eva?'

'No, we weren't close. He was about to leave high school as I was just starting there. I guess I was his irritating little sister.'

I laugh. 'Me and Jude were always together at school. Some classes we separated for as we grew older but we were a team, always waiting to get back to each other. And no one really knew the horrors that were going on when we were at home except us. We were too scared of what Ian would do if we spoke out, and we didn't want to get Mum into trouble. We were always hoping Ian would be like your dad and just leave, but he never did.'

'I can't begin to imagine how painful it must have been for you,' Eva says.

'When Jude died, I thought I'd die too. I didn't think I could breathe without him. I was incomplete. There was no one who could comfort me like my brother. He was my rock and I was his. He was my alibi and I was his. He was my soulmate and I was his. No one gave a thought to how being separated from him made me feel.'

I stop for a moment, feeling a dark cloud looming. But I want to talk. Suddenly I need to tell Eva how I feel about everything. I release a sob as I struggle with the emotions rising up inside of me but I have to keep going.

'No one cared about me. They just wanted to palm me off with another service, so I would become someone else's problem.'

'Maybe that's how you'd see it as a child, but—'

'I never wanted to be with other people. It had always been me and Jude. I was lonely without him, but I felt like the odd one out when I was at school. I was different from the other kids. And the worst thing was, I ruined every relationship I had because I was looking for his replacement. I would find someone who was really nice to me and I would turn him away, because I would either be violent towards him, too clingy, obsessive about getting close, questioning his every move when we weren't together. Like when I was with Scott. I loved him so much, but it was as if I was trying to create this equal of me, so that I could feel whole again. I missed Jude so much and I couldn't move on.'

'Who's Scott?'

'I don't want to talk about him.'

Silence.

'Did you have any counselling?' Eva asks.

'Yes, but it never worked. I would sit in silence for the most part. Doctors and psychiatrists would say I was hard to get to, but I wasn't really. I was a mixed-up kid who had seen her brother murdered, and afterwards, taken away from everything she knew. Imagine that as a child. No one understood what had happened to us as well as Jude did. When he died, I had no one to talk to, to trust, to laugh with, to smile with. To sleep safe with. All I had was wiped out on that day. I wanted Jude to have what I should have, too. Freedom. Food. Love. They weren't much to ask for.

'I remember cuddling up together in my bed. We mostly spent time on one or the other. Both Jude and I were small for our age. Our teachers must have noticed, though were unable to do anything about it. Or they were unwilling – I don't know, but the list for who to abduct was a mile long. I could have chosen so many more. I could have kept going for ages, until I was caught.

But that didn't interest me. What I want is for everyone to know our story. Me and my twin. What really happened to us. I can make it less gruesome if you like?'

'I can write as much or as little as you wish,' Eva says. 'Perhaps you can decide when you read it back? For what it's worth, I think you were both strong to go through what you did as children. During the court trial, I read things I was able to see and remember being shocked at what had happened. It was devastating that Jude couldn't be saved. We live in a society where the weak and the damaged go unmonitored. Usually the only time anyone hears about someone being ill-treated is when something goes wrong. So many children are invisible in the system.'

'Too right. But *I* won't be invisible for much longer. Tell me, Eva – what's your favourite chocolate treat?'

AUGUST 2019

CHAPTER FIFTY

Alison Green

Alison Green sat in her car, reading the *Stoke News* headlines. Goosebumps broke out all over her skin, and she tried not to cry as a rush of adrenaline came at her. She couldn't believe what had happened. Another woman had gone missing, and it was someone she had met.

She had spoken to Eva Farmer three times over the past few months. Alison had first been interviewed after she was released from her captor in May. Even then, Eva had a sympathetic ear and had shown empathy towards her. Because of this, Alison had agreed to be featured again when she'd approached her to run a follow-up article last month.

Of course, she hadn't told the journalist everything but, then again, she wasn't sure she could. She'd told the police most of what happened, but some of it had been too degrading. She hadn't wanted them to know. It had the makings of a horror movie.

Alison had been so affected by the abduction that she hadn't been comfortable mentioning half of what she'd been through. When she had first met Eva, her words had come so quickly that it was almost as if she'd had verbal diarrhoea. Eva must have found it hard to keep up as she'd been writing notes.

Reading the article about Eva brought back vivid memories. The police had been alerted by her husband, David, when she'd failed to return from the supermarket. All Alison could recollect was getting off the bus nearby and yet never getting home.

She and David had two teenage daughters who were still worried about her even now. As a family, they were trying to settle back into normal life, hoping to forget. Natalie was eighteen and due to start at Leeds University. Rebecca was twenty and working as a customer relations supervisor in a large chain of hotels. Alison and David were proud of them both.

Alison recalled quite vividly how much she'd feared for her life during those ten days. Every single second of every long minute of every waking hour. She'd counted them down as best she could, but she'd got lost towards the end. So when she came around outside on day ten, she wasn't sure at first if she was dreaming.

It had been the noise that made her think that something was different. She could hear traffic, smell the fumes from passing vehicles. She'd looked around to find herself in a shop doorway. She remembered glancing up at someone walking past, but they couldn't see her.

The fuzziness in her brain had meant she'd sat for a few minutes trying to figure out what had happened. Then she'd dragged herself up and out onto the pavement to beg for help. Puddles had glistened on the tarmac as she'd pulled the sheet she was wrapped in closer around her body. Her feet had been cold. Looking down at them, she found they were bare.

It was only later, when a woman had stopped to help her, and she was placed in the back of an ambulance by a kindly paramedic, that she realised she was wearing no clothes. She had been so vulnerable out on the streets, but thankfully, it seemed she hadn't been there long. Which still made Alison wonder why he'd wanted her to be found.

It had to be someone evil, someone cruel. Someone who they'd missed. She and David had started fostering when, after complications with the birth of their second daughter, Alison was unable to have any more children. It had devastated them both. They each came from large families so, after a while, they decided to try fostering.

They'd thought of adopting, at first, but as they had two girls already, as a family it seemed kinder to have children on a temporary basis. Fostering meant looking after children when they were at their most vulnerable. Some needed more attention than others.

Young boys and girls had come to their family home whenever they were able to accommodate them. A phone call – can you help – and someone in need would stay for a few days, weeks, occasionally months until they were moved on. Over the years they'd fostered over thirty children, and they'd assumed there were many more to come.

It was no mean feat at times. Some of the children were trouble from the get-go, others were so quiet they hardly knew they were there. But they'd been in this for the long haul. Those kids needed to feel loved by someone, if only for a short time.

But she couldn't think of any one of them who would hate her that much. She and her family had been good to those kids. She'd loved having them around, and it often broke her heart when one of them left. She tried not to get too attached, and she and David had spoken about adopting one or two who had stolen their hearts. But in the end they'd decided they needed space for the temporary kids. It was what they excelled in: helping lost souls find their way again.

It had been stopped now, temporarily, but Alison couldn't see herself as being capable of doing the job she loved any longer.

She and David had done a good job. So it pained her to think it might have been one of them who would have done that to her.

DAY 7

19 August 2019

CHAPTER FIFTY-ONE

Eva

Eva was desperate to get her notes down and done for today. It was hard to keep up with Alex's wandering thoughts, as she frequently went off on a tangent.

Everything was rushing around her head and she wanted time to think. Through the newspaper articles she'd seen, and after hearing about Alison Green, she was convinced the link was what the police had thought: Alex was someone who they'd all dealt with. She'd fooled them all by being quiet, going unnoticed. No wonder none of them had considered it could be her.

Eva's eyes brimmed with tears when she thought of the obvious. If no one suspected Alex, no one would be coming for her either.

All that talk about Alex growing up without Jude had made her think of Daniel. They too had missed out on weddings, children, family get-togethers. She hadn't thought about anything like that until now, supposing she'd just blanked him out of her life purposely. Daniel might be married, with children of his own. She might be an auntie. She should have tried harder to get on with him.

An involuntary shiver ran up her spine as she became aware of her surroundings, troubled by what she was up against. Did the police even have an idea Alex was a woman?

Eva heard the door upstairs open and footsteps coming down the stairs. She hadn't expected Alex to visit until the evening after their chat first thing. Really, she was done for the day: tired and exhausted. So she waited until she was spoken to this time. Even so, she needed to empathise with her, but she was dreading talking to her.

'Eva, speak to me. It's your turn now. Tell me about your brother.'

'I don't want to talk about him.'

'You don't have any choice.'

'Of course I do. You can't take everything from me. I don't have to do as you say.'

'Fine, then you'll go hungry. I don't care.'

'Don't be so childish.'

'You're the one who thinks she can—'

'I've had enough of this,' Eva cried out suddenly. Despite her earlier intentions, she was sick of playing games. 'What kind of fucked-up human being are you to keep me in this room? You need to let me go.'

'Don't tell me what to do.'

'But can't you see how wrong it is? By keeping me here, you're doing yourself no favours for when you do release me.'

'Who says I'll do that?'

'Oh, you will. Because you know you have everyone's attention right now. They're waiting for day ten, to see if I'm released. And my-my husband and my friends will be expecting to hear news.'

'Of you, yes, but not of me. Or maybe they will.' A giggle.

'It's not all about you,' Eva screamed. She pressed her back into the wall and hugged her knees. 'I have been here for seven days. I have eaten your shitty food. I haven't had a wash, and I'm wearing your clothes and they're so filthy and I stink. I never know what time it is. My hair needs washing, that's if you don't cut it all off before beating me black and blue. So you've done a great job of making me feel invisible, but enough is enough. You want me to write this story? Fine. You've made your point. Just let me out.'

'No.'

'Then I won't take any more notes for you.'

'I can get anyone to type out your words. Don't play games with me.'

'I'm not.'

'I will decide whether to let you out or not. My life is in your hands. Do not mess with me. And, quite frankly, you're acting like a spoiled brat, so you should be punished and I—'

'Punished?' Eva couldn't help herself. 'What kind of freak are you? Keeping women, who've done nothing to you, prisoner for ten days and then cutting their hair, dumping them somewhere they won't get seen. Is it going to stop at me, or have you started to have so much fun that you'll continue, despite thinking you can give in? Everyone is waiting for your next move. Does that feel powerful to you?'

'Yes, I'm not invisible any more. And I like that. Soon everyone will know my name.'

'Not from me. You can tell the media yourself. I'm done with you. I'm tired of this. I want to go home.'

'You will do as I say.'

Eva could hear the anger building up in Alex, but she didn't care. 'I said I'm done.'

'I'll tell you when this is finished.'

'Leave me alone.' Eva climbed onto the mattress and pulled the sheet over her head.

'Eva? Eva? Don't ignore me.'

'Just go.'

'No, not until—'

'Will you fuck off and leave me alone!'

The silence that followed was resounding. A ringing in her ears as blood rushed to her head.

No reply came from Alex. A few seconds later, Eva heard footsteps going up the steps and a door slam. She sobbed loudly, relieved it was over for now. Being amicable to get out of here was one thing, but she was weary of being kept like an animal, scared that she wouldn't be getting out on day ten.

Yet her outburst was worrying her, and whether or not she'd be punished for it. Why couldn't she stick to her plan?

She was starting to mirror Alex's actions. One minute she was calm and level-headed, the next she was so out of control it scared her.

She didn't like it. What was happening to her?

CHAPTER FIFTY-TWO

Alex

I go into the living room, slam the door behind me and throw myself on the settee. I pummel the cushion and scream into it silently.

Who does Eva think she is giving me demands? She's locked in that room for one reason: she has to realise how it feels to be invisible. To be treated like an animal. To get no love, no affection. To be ignored. To be dirty, smelly and hungry. Sure she can tell me that's how she feels now, but I get to say when she's released.

These women need to go through what I am doing to them, so they can understand exactly what it's like to be degraded, unloved, unseen and forgotten. Eva is not going to make me feel guilty. I will limit her food this evening. It will serve her right.

The doorbell rings. I check my watch: half past four. I peep out from the side of the bay window, my shoulders dropping when I see it is Milly. I sigh, hoping that I can get rid of her without rousing suspicion.

'Milly!' I smile as I open the front door. 'I didn't realise you were visiting today. What a surprise. Come in.'

'We were meeting for coffee? I waited at the café for half an hour, and when you didn't show I was worried.'

'Oh.' I slap my hand to my forehead, more out of frustration. I was supposed to have sent a message to say that meeting up was out of the question this week. 'I'm so sorry. I forgot the time. I've been reading. I thought it was tomorrow for some reason.'

'No, it was definitely today.'

I hide my annoyance, knowing I'll have to ask her to stay now. Typical.

'I have some chocolate brownies. Would you like one?'

'Ooh, yes please.' Milly removes her jacket.

'How are things?' I engage in small talk.

'Fine. How about you?'

'Good. I just have a lot on at work.' I flick on the kettle. 'I'm so sorry not to have been there for you, Mils. I just lost track of time.'

'That's okay.'

'Have you heard from Jaimie?'

'No, but listen to this. You know over the holidays, I've been hanging around with two girls who I really like and it seems they like me too. Well, today I found out the best news ever. Jaimie is moving schools from September!'

'Serves her right, stupid bitch.'

'Pardon?'

'Oh, nothing.' I wave away her comment. 'That's great news.'

Milly picks up the book we were reading last week, and we discuss our likes and dislikes for the next ten minutes. To be honest, it stills my mind and I'm actually glad Milly has called. All that talk about Jude today has unsettled me more than I imagined it would.

'Are you going to show me your writing some time soon?' I ask her then.

Milly titters. 'No way. But I'm enjoying it. It's about a serial killer.'

'Ooh, dark!' I laugh.

'It's not too violent. More psychological, I think… what's that noise?'

I hear a distinct tapping and groan inwardly.

'What noise?' I say, pretending I can't hear anything.

'That banging. Don't you hear it?'

'It's just the radiators.' I shake my head and get to my feet quickly. 'Let's play some tunes. What do you fancy?'

I switch on the TV and choose a music channel. While we dance around the kitchen, I fume inwardly. The noise is coming from downstairs. Eva must have heard us talking and is trying to get our attention. The last time that happened was when Alison Green began to scream and bang when the meter reader came into the house. Luckily for her, he hadn't suspected anything, but I did take my anger out on her once I'd drugged her that night.

I will have to control my temper and try not to do the same to Eva once Milly has gone.

CHAPTER FIFTY-THREE

Eva

Devastated that no one had reacted to her banging, Eva sat on the mattress and rested her chin on her knees. She knew someone had called to see Alex, was often under the assumption that there was another person in on the abduction with her. Now she'd be in for it if Alex was annoyed.

Since her refusal to talk, she'd been left alone for hours. She'd smelt food earlier and could smell it again. Her stomach growled in protest. So she was glad to hear footsteps coming down the stairs.

The hatch was opened, and she could hear giggling as Alex stooped down to her level.

'You're going to love this evening's meal,' Alex told her, pushing the tray through.

Eva could see a bowl of pasta bolognese and a chunk of garlic bread. But as soon as she moved towards it, the tray was dragged back out of the room.

'Hey, wait,' she cried.

'Do you think you deserve anything after your little tantrum earlier, and then the banging on the door? Tut tut. I don't think so. What do I have to do to get you to behave today?' Alex sighed dramatically.

'I'm sorry, okay! Please, I need to eat.'

'Pity.'

Eva tried not to imagine the food going into her mouth instead of Alex's as she heard the fork scraping on the plate. The smell was divine; her mouth watered and her stomach lurched as she understood that nothing was coming to her.

'This is delicious.' Alex laughed. 'Even if I do say so myself. I cooked it from scratch to use everything up in the cupboards. I've become quite a dab hand in the kitchen.'

Eva moved back to sit on the mattress. It was so hot in the room, sweat beading all over her body. She needed a drink. She'd beg if she had to, but not yet.

'If you want to eat tonight, you need to talk to me,' Alex said. 'If you want me to talk as well, then I have to know what happened to you after your dad murdered your mum.'

There was no point in refusing this time. Because of what Alex had told her so far, Eva knew she'd done her research, but that wouldn't mean she'd know everything. And she might get away with talking about Daniel for now.

'I've already told you. Daniel and I went to live with my aunt and uncle,' she said.

'And how did you feel about that?'

'I thought it was the best thing all round.'

'Lucky you.'

'It didn't feel like it. I missed my mum.'

'I hate mine.'

'Do you still go and see her?'

'In prison?'

'Yes.'

'She came out last year.'

'Oh.'

'You didn't know?'

'No.'

'Then you weren't keeping an eye on me as much as you thought you were.'

'I'm sorry.' Eva was getting good at lying now.

'No, you're not. What about your brother? Are you close to him?'

'No.'

'Would you like to be?'

'There's too much water under the bridge. He was sixteen when it happened, and he left to join the army shortly afterwards. We grew apart.'

'Is that why you're so close to Nick?'

'Nick's my husband. It's a totally different thing.'

'But you love him very much, don't you? Just like you love your brother.'

Eva clammed up then. It had been leading up to this, talking about Daniel, and she wanted to barter information so that she could find out more about Scott. Yet she couldn't do it – not tonight.

'Do you want children, Eva?'

Eva drew in a breath. Was Alex asking her a genuine question or had she guessed what she was hiding from her?

No, she wouldn't know. Perhaps she'd assumed Eva had been sick with a reaction to the sedatives in her food and drink. Eva had to play carefully now not to give herself away.

'Yes, I'd like one or two, if possible.'

'I'm surprised you haven't started trying. At your age, you're leaving it late. I suppose you're a career couple.' Alex scoffed.

'We want to be settled financially before starting a family.'

'What would you like? A girl or a boy?'

'I have no preference as long as it's healthy.'

'Oh, aren't you the typical woman.' Snide laughter this time.

'Alex, I feel so weak. If I'm not getting food, then I'm going to sleep,' she said.

'You're dismissed when I tell you. Why won't you talk about your brother?'

'I won't bow down to your every request.'

'Then you'll just have to starve. You're in my control, don't forget that. Your life is in my hands.'

Life. Eva pressed a hand to her stomach.

'I'm sorry,' she replied. 'What do you want to know?'

'Tell me about the night it happened.'

'Please. I—'

'Tell me!'

'Okay, okay! It was—'

'I'm bored with you now. You can tell me tomorrow.'

The tray was slid through the hatch again. Eva jumped up quickly, disappointed when she saw the delicious-smelling food had been swapped for her usual meal. Still, she took it eagerly. She didn't care that she would gag as she ate the food, and that the tea would be cold by now. She just needed nourishment.

The hatch banged shut. And just like that, day seven was over.

Once she'd eaten, and drank, Eva crawled into bed and tried to get some sleep. But she tossed and turned while she waited for the sedative to work.

In the end, she sat up and looked ahead. The room was still fairly light. Before she fell asleep, she imagined shadows jumping out at her, things she didn't want to see, and yet if she closed her eyes, it was the same.

She wondered if she had the strength to get to the end.

And then she thought of how much she wanted to be with Nick. Usually crying gave her relief. It was an outlet for the fear, the anger, the anxiety. But here in this room, it made her seem weak. As if she was giving away far too much of herself, a side that she didn't want to reveal.

She had to keep thinking there was not long to go now.

DAY 8

20 August 2019

CHAPTER FIFTY-FOUR

Eva

Eva woke up, unable to comprehend another day alone in the cellar. A sense of dread hung over her all the time. What would happen with Alex? What would she learn? What would she have to share?

As she used the bucket, she saw it was still full. Alex hadn't come into her room last night. Strangely, it made her feel more alone than ever.

Trying not to think of Nick made her realise the other things she was missing: her weekly meet-up with her friend, Shona; the breakfast they used to enjoy from their local farm shop. Nipping to the shop around the corner from the office for a chocolate run. Her news team, the office, the noise, the banter. The excitement of breaking news. The horror of real life.

She yearned for material things like her phone and her laptop. Driving home in her car. Netflix and a good mug of tea. Reading the book she'd been halfway through. Her own clothes, clean and fitting.

Her sense of identity. Her freedom.

She missed everything really. How could she not?

So when she heard the door to the stairs opening, she sat behind the hatch in anticipation of her next visit.

'What do you want to know from me today?' she asked as soon as it was opened.

'Patience, Eva. First you must eat.'

The tray slid in, and she scrambled off the mattress. She grabbed at the toast and shoved it in her mouth, trying not to eat it too quickly. Then she sipped at the tea, hot for once.

She closed her eyes and pulled up an image of her and Nick in the kitchen. What she would do to be at home eating breakfast with him right now. She had to hold on to that thought. It would help to get her through the day.

Two slices of toast was hardly a meal but at least it was something. Instead, she imagined it was a Staffordshire oatcake, filled with crispy bacon and cheese and slathered in tomato sauce. Perhaps a mushroom or two. It would fill her for the next couple of hours and, hopefully, she would get some sleep before the hunger pains became too much.

'What's your favourite wine, Eva?'

Eva frowned. First Alex wanted to know what flowers she liked, then chocolate and now wine. Was she planning a last supper for her?

'Eva?'

'I prefer red,' she replied. 'A nice Merlot.'

'Me too – snap! We've become quite friendly over the past few days, don't you think?'

'Yes,' Eva lied, trying not to laugh out of frustration. The woman didn't know the meaning of the word.

'So don't you think it's about time we told each other the truth?'

'What do you mean?'

'Well, I've been thinking about your story. There must be a reason you don't want to stay in touch with your brother, or talk about him. I would have assumed after something so tragic happening you'd be close to him. So the only conclusion I can come to is you're protecting him for some reason.'

Eva closed her eyes, trying to rid herself of the memories that she had pushed away for years.

*

Eva had been ill with a tummy infection and at home from school. She was in her room underneath her duvet, feeling sorry for herself after throwing up for most of the night and into the morning.

Her mum came into her room that afternoon. She'd made her some toast and a cup of tea, hoping to get her to eat. She'd sat with Eva for a few moments and then left her when there had been a knock at the door.

It took Eva a few seconds to register the noise. There was shouting, an angry deep voice alongside her mum. Then there was a scream and a loud sound, like a slap to her skin.

Eva had frozen for a moment, unsure what to do. But then she'd come to her senses and raced out of her room and down the stairs.

Her mum was on the living room floor, her arms flailing. She was hitting out at her dad as he held her down. It was then she saw the knife in his hand, saw it going in and out of her mum's body.

As he drew it back to inflict another wound, she screamed and raced at him. 'Stop it,' she cried.

It had the desired effect of bringing him out of his trance. He stepped away as far as he could until his back hit the windowsill. Then he dropped the knife.

'What have I done?' he said quietly. 'What have I done?'

Eva cradled her mum's head on her knees, unsure what to do. Blood poured from her mum's body at an alarming rate from the puncture wounds all over her chest and stomach. Eva lost count at ten. She looked at her father in disbelief.

She remembered all the times he'd been abusive towards her mother. The evenings he'd come home drunk and picked a fight so that he could hit her and then say it was her fault. The mornings she'd seen a new bruise on her mum's arm or caught her wincing as she'd clutched at her chest. The nights he'd not come home after taking all the money they had in the house – even what had been in her piggy bank – to go and get drunk.

For twelve months, life had been good without him around.

And then, just like that, in a minute or two, life as Eva had known it was over. Her mum was gone.

'Eva,' he said, holding out his bloodied hands to his sides. 'I'm so sorry.'

Eve stepped towards the knife.

The front door opened and Daniel came bounding in. Eva stopped what she was doing immediately.

'What's going on?' Daniel looked at his mum, his dad, his sister and then the knife on the floor. 'Is she…?' he asked Eva.

'I-I don't know.' Eva nodded regardless.

'I'm sorry, son.'

Daniel ignored his father and dropped to the floor next to Eva. 'Get the phone,' he told her.

Eva did as she was told and passed it to him. Daniel had removed his blazer and shirt and was wrapping them around Mum's body. Eva listened as he told the emergency services she'd been attacked by their father.

All the while, Dad just stood there in a daze, eyes wide.

In one quick movement, Daniel reached for the knife.

'You bastard,' he cried.

Eva watched in horror as Daniel drew back his hand and pushed it into his father's chest, twisting it up further.

She screamed as their father's face contorted, the colour disappearing from his cheeks as he dropped to the floor, never to get up again. She still had nightmares about it now.

Before anyone arrived, Eva and Daniel made a pact to say their dad had killed their mum before turning the knife on himself. But Daniel's life had gone wrong with the guilt of what he'd done, and Eva had found it hard to stay close to him.

She'd blamed herself for what had happened for years afterwards. If only she'd come downstairs earlier, she might have stopped her dad before it was too late.

If only her dad wasn't such a drunken, violent bastard.

If only…

Daniel hadn't joined the army, as she'd told Alex. He'd left as soon as he'd finished school, gone down south for work. But he'd contacted her recently, through the *Stoke News* at first. He'd emailed her often, saying he wanted to talk.

Eva had thought there was nothing to say. Until now.

*

'Eva, answer my question,' Alex said. 'Are you protecting him?'

'No, I'm not,' she lied, determined to keep something back from Alex. 'It's just painful to talk about.'

'It won't take long.'

Eva said nothing, hoping Alex would leave her alone. But she wasn't expecting what was to come.

'You know the red mist descending, Eva, making your dad do unthinkable things?' Alex said. 'Well, that happened to me too. It's about time I told you about Scott.'

CHAPTER FIFTY-FIVE

Alex

I make myself as comfortable as possible on the floor. I am going to enjoy sharing this story.

'Three years ago, I met Scott. I was working in a computer shop. He came in because his laptop had broken. I told him it would take a week to repair. He didn't want to leave it that long. I wasn't really supposed to, but the manager was off that afternoon, so I told him I could fix it for him, if we kept it between ourselves. I'd been to college to study IT. I have a knack of being able to mend things and had started taking on the odd job at the shop.

'Scott said if I could do it for him quicker than that, he would take me out to dinner to say thanks. I said I wanted paying for the job. He'd laughed and said that was a given. He wanted to take me out as well. I was flattered. He was so good-looking, dark, like me, with the same colour eyes. He reminded me of Jude and, at the time, I realised that was good. Turned out it was the worst thing ever for Scott.'

'I don't understand,' Eva replies.

'We hit it off after that first day and quickly became a couple, then we moved in together. The first few months were okay, but then my head started going funny. When Jude died, I had no one. People addressed the fact that my mum and Ian had killed him, and I was left an orphan. But what they didn't help me with was the grief of losing my other half.

'I researched about twinless-twins after I left Scott. It helped me understand what happened to him. What I did.'

'What do you mean?'

'We were happy at first,' I go on, ignoring her question. 'And then, I don't really know what happened but I wanted him to change. I needed him to be more like me. He was quite independent, and I was possessive over him. Obsessive, I think, might seem more appropriate. It drove Scott mad and we began arguing a lot. In the end, he told me he couldn't go on like this and he was leaving. And like your dad, I saw red and picked up a knife.'

'You stabbed him?'

I can hear the shock in Eva's voice, the fear as she recognises how much she is at my mercy. It is very exciting.

'Not that time,' I tease.

'I still don't understand.'

'You don't need to.' I check my watch and stretch my arms above my head. 'I have to make a move. I can't sit around talking to you all morning. I have plans. But before I leave, I'm going to let you in on a secret. It's about woman number four. I thought you might like to know that she's still here.'

I hear Eva gasp, and I grin. That got her attention.

'Do you believe me, Eva?'

'Yes, I believe you.'

'Good, because I want you to write about it. If I tell you what happened to her, will you?'

'What happened to her?' Eva repeats.

'Do you think Jillian is still alive? Or do you think she's dead?'

'She preferred to be called Jill. I knew her.'

'Oh! Was she your bestest-friend-forever?'

'No, I didn't see her often but our husbands worked at the same station.'

'Interesting. Did you get on with her?'

'She's one of the people I love to be around. She's kind, always willing to help, thoughtful too. She roots for the underdog, always going the extra mile to help people.'

'She didn't do that with me. Have you finished your drink yet? Because I need you to write this down.'

'Yes.'

I hear Eva turning over a page in her notebook.

'She was one of the officers who came to the house when my brother died.'

'Are you sure?'

I frown. 'Are you doubting me?'

'No, I—'

'I remember every single one of the people who should have looked after me and didn't. They've haunted my dreams for years. Jill should have done more for me. I wanted to talk to her but she wouldn't listen.'

'What is it that you wanted to tell her?'

'How badly Ian treated us. I hadn't told anyone what we'd been through since he'd moved in with us. But I needed someone to know, to understand me. Even to hug me and say it was all going to be okay. I was young, Jude had died, and yet she didn't give me the time of day.'

'I'm sure she would have done everything she could had she known. It must have been a very busy time,' she says.

'She should have *made* time for me. They all should have.'

'Is Jill still here?' Eva asks.

'Yes.'

'Is she—?'

I hear Eva sob, so I put her out of her misery.

'Yes, Eva,' I say. 'Jill is dead.'

CHAPTER FIFTY-SIX

Eva

Eva's mind went into overdrive. She held in a sob as she thought of her friend. Was Alex telling the truth this time or was Jill in another room? Were they being held captive together with only a few walls between them?

She rushed over to the bucket and threw up. Tears stung her eyes for Jill, and for herself. She was no longer able to work out the truth from the lies. But she was ready to humour Alex all the same.

'I didn't mean to kill her,' Alex went on. 'I just gave her too much of the drug, and she never woke up. It messed up my plans but I compromised. Having easy access to you was ideal, and I was able to bring everything under control in time. That's why I need you to tell my story. Everyone has to know why before I disappear. Because they will blame me for what happened.'

Eva squeezed her eyes tightly shut, pushing out all the visions that were flying through her mind. Alex was talking about her friend as if she was a nothing. No one of importance. But she was to her. And didn't Alex realise she was responsible for everything, not just Jill's death, if that was true?

Why had she assumed Alex would release her after ten days? It was purely a game to her.

'I thought I gave her the right dose of the drug before I released her,' Alex went on. 'I watched her on the camera drinking it all and then eating her food. But when I went down to her, she was slumped on the bed. I shook her, but she didn't wake up. And when I pressed on her neck for a pulse, I couldn't find one. I must have measured the dosage wrong. Or she mustn't have been able to handle it like the other women. I don't know.

'I couldn't even call for help: *999 emergency, I have a woman who's been held captive for ten days. I've just given her a drug to make her more accommodating. I must have given her too much because now she's dead.* Not sure that would have worked in my favour.'

Eva shivered when she heard manic laughter. How did Alex manage to move from nice to nasty within a few seconds? She couldn't get her head around which Alex she was dealing with at the best of times. It was frightening to think she might give her the same drink soon.

'I know what you're thinking, and you will drink yours when it's time. Otherwise you won't get out. And neither will you have any food or water while I think what to do with you. Taking the drink is imperative for your escape, and don't forget that. I'm the one who's in charge here, do you understand?'

Eva couldn't find her voice at first, afraid that Alex might guess what she was thinking again. 'I do,' she replied eventually, in a whisper that was barely there.

'Good.'

She heard Alex moving, realising she was getting to her feet.

'I didn't mean to kill your friend. You do believe me, don't you?'

'Yes,' she lied.

'Good girl. Right, I'm off. I have things to do. It's going to be a fun day.' Alex's laughter filled the room until she was gone.

Eva wasn't sure she should continue with these games now she knew she might not get home. What was the point? But then she pressed a hand to her stomach. She couldn't care less about being two-faced.

She held everything in until she heard Alex's footsteps disappear and the door close behind her. Then she let out a silent scream.

CHAPTER FIFTY-SEVEN

Alex

After I've been to see Eva, I throw myself down onto the settee and laugh. I wish I could have seen her face when I told her about Jillian. And the best thing is she won't know whether to believe me or not. I mean, I'm not sure she'd doubt me, but she doesn't really know me well enough to know if I'm lying or telling the truth.

My laugh becomes hysterical as I think of her stuck in my cellar, knowing her friend is dead and that her fate is in my hands. It's almost primal the power I feel when I'm in control this way. Eva is at my mercy now. I can do whatever I want to her. She has no say over her life.

Of course, I didn't plan to do that to Jillian. Everything I said to Eva was true. I must have messed up with the dose of sedative. And I was really looking forward to torturing Jill before I let her go. I had decided to shave her head and make her tattoo larger and more noticeable. I was getting more confident by number four. So it had been a bitter blow when I found her dead.

Burying her had taken its toll on me. I don't have a large area here, but there is a grass patch at the rear of the garden, down the side of a dilapidated shed. It's a way from the house but I was able to drag Jill's body down during the night and bury her when everyone was asleep.

Digging the hole had been strenuous, and dangerous too, as I could be seen during the day. So I dug a little every night for three nights and then buried her on the fourth, while I watched everyone getting in a frenzy because she hadn't come home as expected.

That's when I was given a name. The Silent Abductor. Now that had been exciting. I was all over the TV and newspapers, national as well as local. It was actually fun coming home from work reading all about it, sitting watching it of an evening before I went out into the garden during the night.

I laugh again. Some of my actions haven't gone to plan, but they have worked out far better in the end.

I really am going to get away with everything. Only two more days to go. And the best fun is about to happen in a couple of hours.

I pull myself up from the settee. I'd better get ready for it.

CHAPTER FIFTY-EIGHT

Eva

Eva sank to the mattress as fear and grief overtook her in equal measure. It was impossible not to react after what Alex had said. Because if Jill Bradshaw was still at the house, it could mean only two things.

The first she hoped and prayed was the one Alex would tell her about soon: that she was lying. Jill would be locked up in another room and still alive.

But she had been missing for weeks, so she would be in a terrible state. And why would Alex keep her there for so long? Why hadn't Jill been released after ten days like the first three women?

The second thing she couldn't bear to think about was that Jill hadn't come home because Alex had killed her. The more she spoke with Alex, the more she realised she seemed quite capable of ending someone's life.

She and Jill had always got on well whenever they spent time together. They'd shared many a meal and the odd glass of wine when someone was retiring from the force or getting married, perhaps celebrating a birthday. She liked her husband too. Steve was a gentle giant of a cop, taller even than Nick. The two of them together reminded her of bouncers on a club door.

Nick thought a lot of Jill too. Even before she'd gone missing, Eva could see the mental strain that had been put on him over the past few months. Someone was abducting women and he, along with many other officers – although doing their jobs – felt like they were failing.

He'd come home one evening looking drained. She'd gone towards him, glad when he wrapped his arms around her and hugged her fiercely.

'There's nothing new,' he told her. 'We have four more days until Jill should be released. We're keeping an eye on places we think she may be dropped off, which are relevant to her, but with no clue to who and why yet, it's a needle in a haystack time.'

'Well, I'll do what I can with the local news, you know that.'

He kissed her forehead, and she looked up, this time seeing the tears in his eyes.

'Hey, you're doing your best,' she soothed. 'Knowing Jill, she'll come back fighting.'

'Let's hope so.'

'Want a bite to eat? Something light – toast perhaps?'

He nodded. 'I've only come home for some shut-eye, as I can't concentrate at the moment without falling asleep.'

'Toast it is. Do you want to shower while I get it made? And tea too?'

'Please.'

She'd watched his gait as he'd walked away that night: the defeated steps of a troubled man. Tears had fallen then, too, as she'd wondered what Jill would be like after ten days of incarceration. But then the worry that she'd be the first woman not to come home had turned into a reality.

If Eva had her phone, she would look back over the article she'd written in July when Jill had first gone missing. From how Alex was reacting, her state of mind seemed to change if she seemed threatened, or thought someone was getting the better of her. Jill was a police officer, trained to deal with people like Alex. Perhaps she'd put up a fight and it had gone wrong.

Now there was no telling if Alex would let Eva go. Maybe she intended on keeping her for longer because she was writing out her story.

Why had she grabbed Alex that day and made her speak? If she hadn't done that, sure she would be going out of her mind, but she would have had a better chance of being released. Now she was at Alex's mercy, and it wasn't a good place to be.

She clutched her chest as her breathing became shallow and painful as she tried to take in air. It wouldn't be the first panic attack she'd had since being locked up, but equally, it could be as dangerous.

'Five, four, three, two, one. Everything is fine,' she repeated. Even Nick's face, memories of time spent with him, didn't alleviate the foreboding she was feeling right then. Eva knew it was day eight from the date on the newspapers she'd been given to read each evening. She couldn't deliberate if she were to be released on day ten. Although she needed to stay positive, she didn't want to think too far ahead for fear of it not coming true.

She didn't want to think of the present either. Alex could come into the cellar any time she liked. For all Eva knew, she might up the dosage of her sleeping medication after she'd reacted angrily earlier.

Would Alex even want anyone to know Eva had helped tell her story once it was finished? Was she being played? It was highly likely. It was hard to distinguish when she hadn't known Alex personally, but she had known Jill. Jill would have helped Alex as much as she could.

No, she couldn't be certain that Alex was telling the truth about Jill. It was so frustrating. She had to stick to her plan. If she did what Alex said, she might release her soon.

But if Alex had killed Jill, then she might kill Eva too.

Eva cried again, her mind going round in circles. She was in a hopeless position. She couldn't defend herself in any way. She didn't even know what she was dealing with.

It was going to be another long day, because she wouldn't believe that Jill was dead until she knew for certain. Her beautiful, kind, articulate friend couldn't have been killed at the hands of a madwoman. She should have asked Alex for more information. This could be a trick she was playing on her.

Yet something told her this time Alex wasn't lying.

Tears of frustration poured out of her. She was exhausted, confused and tired of questioning everything. Alex had told her so many things that she wasn't sure anything could be true. It couldn't be.

Eva lay down on the mattress, curled up in the foetal position, her hand to her stomach. There was no doubt in her mind that Alex had got one thing wrong. Because Jill couldn't have been the police officer that arrested Ian Carrington after little Jude's murder. Jill hadn't joined the police force until ten years ago.

Which meant that Alex had abducted, possibly murdered, the wrong person.

CHAPTER FIFTY-NINE

Alex

In the kitchen, I watch Eva on the monitor. She seems genuinely upset. Like I care. She hasn't had to suffer through life like me. Okay, we did have similar tragedies, but she landed on her feet. How can that be fair?

I glance at the clock: better start getting things ready.

First I prepare Eva's drink for that evening. I undo the top of the bottled water and tip a few centimetres down the sink. I take the Rohypnol and pour it into the water. I don't need to do much more than that as the liquid is colourless and odourless.

I know from experience how damaging taking Rohypnol long-term can be. I was under its influence when I was with Scott. It wasn't entirely my fault. He'd introduced me to it. He had said it would give a high that I'd love, alongside taking alcohol. He said it would dull my mind, take away my pain. Which it did, but it also made me unpredictable.

I've been off the stuff for about a year, knowing I wouldn't be able to carry out my plan under its influence. While I need to be alert all the time, I don't care about its effects on Eva.

I suppose the dosage depends on each individual's shape and size, not to mention demeanour. But this time I'm going to be careful. I don't want Eva to die before I've had my fun. I was robbed of my chance to get that part of my plan in the newspaper, as I was unable to release Jillian.

It's nearly half past eleven already. I start to prepare lunch.

*

Upstairs, afterwards, I sit for a moment on my bed. I can feel everything brewing up inside me and, as much as I want to release the anger, it isn't a good sign. The pain, the hurt, the image of that bastard in my head. I wrestle with my rage at the thought of what I could have done to him had he not been killed in prison.

Justice was never served on Ian. Some might say he got what he deserved, but I don't. I wish he'd completed his full sentence so he could be beaten week after week. Prisoners don't like child murder cases.

I wanted someone to hold his head under water in a toilet until he almost drowned, and then repeat the procedure.

I wanted a prisoner to flog him with whatever metal piping they could get hold of. He warranted so much more pain than the two years he got.

I shake away the melancholy and move to the window. Outside, it's quiet. There are a few parked cars but most people are out at work. It's not a busy place at this end of the road, apart from when the kids are playing football on the green at the side and that's mostly bearable.

I turn to go for a shower. But then I sweep everything off my dressing table onto the floor in one almighty roar.

Downstairs, I check the oven to see the tuna pasta bake I've made is coming on nicely. It's all I have in so it will have to do.

While the food is cooking, I set about getting what I need ready. I lay the sharp scissors on the table. Then I place the nail clippers alongside them. Next is the tattoo gun. I'm getting quite good at doing them now: I take a biro downstairs with me and draw a number on the side of the women's necks and then I tattoo over it. It's the part I enjoy most. Branding them for life. And once that's done, I can get rid of any final pent-up frustration. I'm sure there'll be lots of it later today.

I'm placing all the items into my holdall when the doorbell rings. I clap my hands with glee, rushing through the hall.

I open the front door. The woman standing on the step smiles. She obviously wants to make a good impression. It's exceptionally warm today, and yet she has a trouser suit on as if she's coming for an interview.

From her demeanour I can see she is agitated. Her eyes are landing everywhere but on me. Behind me, to the side, at me for a second and then to the floor.

I wait for her to look at me again, and then I plaster a smile on my face to greet the woman I hate so much.

'Hello, Mum.'

CHAPTER SIXTY

Alex

I've been waiting for this day for thirteen years and, now it's here, I can't contain my excitement. She's obviously changed quite a bit since I last saw her, but she hasn't aged well at all. Her hair is short, almost grey all over, and even though she wears a little make-up, she seems pale. Mind, that might be to do with the fact she's been in prison for eleven years.

'Is it okay to call you Mum?' I ask.

'Yes, of course.' Maria Dixon steps inside at my beckoning.

'Did it take you long to get here?'

'No, it was fine.'

'Let me take your jacket and then I'll get us a drink.'

'I brought you these.' Maria holds out her hand, the handle of a carrier bag wrapped within her fist.

I take it from her and peek inside. 'Ooh, chocolates and wine. You shouldn't have.'

'I wasn't sure whether you preferred red or white, so I bought one of each.'

Maria shrugs off her jacket. I hang it up for her. It's a cheap make, I notice from the label. Well-worn too. I wonder if it's second-hand.

I smile and point to a door. 'Go through into the living room and I'll be with you in a moment.'

I march into the kitchen and close the door behind me. I need a breather. My heart is booming out of my chest but I want to relish this day, to savour every minute of it. I've been planning it for so long. Every detail has to be right. I am going to show Maria Dixon that I've coped very well, despite what happened to me because of her.

I can hear banging from downstairs and groan inwardly. Eva is trying to get attention again. I turn on the radio and leave it on loud enough to drown the noise out and go back to join my mother in the living room.

Maria is standing by the fireplace. We sit down and after a little stilted conversation, I get to my feet again. 'I think the food will be ready soon. Would you like to sit at the table and I'll pour wine? Which would you prefer?'

'I haven't got a preference. Since being in prison, I'm happy with what I get.'

Maria is smiling so I giggle. But I don't find it funny in the slightest. She was in that place because of what she'd done to Jude.

Jude.

I'm doing this for him, and yet I can barely recall his face when I think of him. I can see him in my mother though. I can see him in her eyes, the shape of her chin. I can see me too.

I shake the anger from my shoulders and dish out the food. The TV is playing low in this room. I have it tuned in to a news channel. It's showing images of Eva again – at work, of her husband and where she was last seen.

'Such a shame about those women going missing, isn't it?' Maria says, tucking into her food.

'Why?' I ask.

'Well, it must be a whacko who can do that to someone. It seems unthinkable.'

'But it was all right for you to do the same to your children?'

'That's not what happened.'

'Really? How is it different?'

'I was… I was mentally ill at that time. I didn't know what I was doing.'

'You were messed up, but you had a voice.'

'I didn't. I was controlled by Ian. He was terrifying when he was in a mood. I had to hide from him lots of times so that he wouldn't beat me. Twice I thought I was going to die.'

'Poor you.' I smile sweetly so she can't make out if I'm being sympathetic or sarcastic. 'Do you think about Jude at all?'

'Of course I do. Every day I have to live with what I did. It's not easy. I still have nightmares about it.'

'Do you see his face? I can't remember what he looks like.'

'I have a few photos of him. Would you like me to bring some with me, if we meet again?'

'Would you like to?'

'Yes. It's been lovely to see what a beautiful woman you've turned into. I can hardly recognise you as my own.' She points at her face. 'My skin is so dull after years locked up with no sunlight.'

'And whose fault is that?'

Maria bends her head for a moment. 'I feel like I stick my foot in it every time I say something. I'm sorry.'

'You will be,' I mutter under my breath as I stand up and collect the plates.

'Sorry, I didn't catch what you said.'

'I said would you like a piece of cake?'

'That would be lovely, thanks.'

I move back into the kitchen and close the door behind me again. I need another moment to compose myself before I lose it altogether. It's proving much harder to be nice than I thought. Still, I wanted to talk to my mother before administering her punishment, so it's time to get going with my plan.

I pour more wine and add Rohypnol to her glass. I give the drink a swirl and then take it through.

'Here you go.' I enter the room with a tray. 'I topped up your wine too.'

'Oh, not for me, thanks.' Maria puts up a hand.

'I'm sure a little more won't hurt.' I smile my encouragement, raising my eyebrows, urging her to drink.

'Oh, go on, then. Thank you.' Maria picks up the glass.

I put the tray on the table and cut two large slices while I wait for the magic to work.

'What do you do for a living now?' I ask. 'Were you able to get a job with your record?'

'I work at the local Co-op. Nothing exciting. What do you do?'

'I'm an IT expert.'

'Sounds like you're very clever. That's beyond me.' She giggles again. 'Do you have any friends around here? Or a boyfriend?'

I keep my sigh to myself, impatient for the drugs to take effect now. Oh, woman, you're such a bore. All the shit you're coming out with – is it to make you feel better? Because it sucks that you think none of this is your fault. You started it all.

But I'm going to finish it.

I wait a little longer for her to begin drifting away. I can see her blinking rapidly, shaking her head slightly as if she wonders what's going on. When I know I have her full attention and that she is no longer capable of stopping me from doing anything, I stand up.

'It took me a while to get to you, obviously, yet you were always part of the plan,' I tell her. 'I knew you'd come and find me one day.'

Maria titters, putting out a hand in front of her. I slap it away and she laughs some more.

'When I got your first email, I didn't know what to expect – a jolt of emotion, perhaps? A surge of rage? Well, I felt neither. What I do recall was the excitement about what was to come.'

'I like your house,' Maria says, looking around the room as she tries to focus.

'Getting you here wasn't hard. You always were gullible, weren't you?'

Maria laughs again.

'I told you I lived in a nice location. I said there were lots of rooms for you to stay. Well, I wasn't lying. I simply forgot to tell you that you'd be locked up in one of them and wouldn't be allowed to leave.'

Maria grins at me. She's having trouble focusing already. It's time to make my move.

'I have a surprise for you.' I pull her up to standing. 'I'm sure you're going to like it.'

'Okay.'

Hearing the slur in her voice, I smile. The drug is taking effect. In a few minutes, Mummy Dear, you will be all in my control. Let the fun begin.

CHAPTER SIXTY-ONE

Alex

I place my holdall over my shoulder. 'Come on,' I say to Maria. 'Let's get you upstairs to bed.'

'What time is it?'

'It's nearly ten o'clock,' I lie. It isn't even half past two this afternoon.

'I can't stay over.' Maria's voice is slow and quiet.

'Oh, I insist.' I help her to her feet again. She's collapsed twice now because she's in such a state. I wrap my arm around her waist and guide her towards the door. 'You're so drunk.' I giggle, wanting to put her at ease for now.

It takes us a few minutes to get upstairs. We're both laughing because she keeps on missing the steps. Rohypnol dosing is such an individual thing. Sometimes, like with Stephanie Harvey, it wasn't enough and I had to give her more the next day. That's why I hadn't been able to release her until the evening of day ten, rather than first thing in the morning.

I push the door to my bedroom open so I can get through with Maria. She's slowly becoming a dead weight. I'll have to hurry or else she'll pass out before I can have my fun.

I sit down on the bed with her. 'Let's get you out of your clothes.'

'Am I staying here tonight?' Maria asks.

I smile. She's already asked me that. The drug is working. 'Yes. I'm going to look after you.'

'You're such a good daughter. I don't deserve you, not after what I did.'

'Oh, don't worry about that now. Come on, let's do your hair first.'

I pull out the scissors and take strands of her hair, the same colour as my own, between my fingers. Then I hack away at it. Maria watches it fall in her lap, not at all bothered.

Next I cut her nails. I'm leaving the tattoo until later. It's the fun part but I don't want her fidgeting. It won't take any more than ten minutes, and I know it doesn't hurt as I've had several inked myself.

I sit back for a moment and admire my handiwork. My mother's hair is a total mess, her nails clipped and painted black. I'm not sure why I started with the varnish but it's become my signature mark now. At least it is quick drying.

'I've been so good to you, Mum,' I tell her. 'I did think of taking you out completely with extra drugs in the wine, but where's the fun in that? I'm afraid I'll have to do the knocking out myself, though. This is the bit I like most.'

As I begin to beat Maria, her screams are loud again. It isn't a problem, though, as it won't be for long and no one will hear her up here. The neighbours are at work and, even if they're in, they'll assume it's something I'm watching on TV, like the last time. Besides, it'll be over if they do come to see what's going on, plus I will have gagged her by then. I just want to have my fun first.

When I've had enough, I take one of her hands and place it inside a handcuff already attached to the headboard. It's one of a pair that you can find in any sex shop – these have red fur around the metal. I push Maria down on the bed and reach for her other arm. She is sobbing quietly now. Her hand clicks into the other cuff, and I laugh.

'We're going to have so much fun this evening,' I say, straightening out Maria's legs. Once her feet are tied together, I sigh. I administer a slap because she's not looking at me. It feels so good.

Maria isn't laughing now. She's not saying anything. Bruising is already appearing on her face.

'When I was seven years old, I came home from school one afternoon with an art project. I had drawn a family portrait. I wanted to make you and Dad happy. I was really proud of it.'

Maria whimpers.

'It was on the kitchen wall for nearly three years before Ian ripped it up and threw it to the floor. "I don't like that, not now I'm here," he'd said. I asked him why not, and he said because my dad was dead. Just like that. He didn't care that he'd ruined a memory, something precious to me. And you never said a word.'

'I'm sorry,' Maria spoke. 'I was scared.'

'Don't you dare blame that bastard for everything! Because you weren't as innocent as you make out to everyone. You enjoyed what you did to us, just as much as he did. And me and Jude suffered because of you.'

'No,' Maria slurs.

'You should have protected us. You should have left Ian and taken us to safety. But oh no – you liked what he was doing. You enjoyed dishing out punishments. So now I think it's time I dished out some of my own.'

'Ian didn't kill Jude,' Maria mumbles. 'It was you.'

'What?' Maria's words pierce my memories. Me and Jude. Jude in my arms after Ian had kicked him. I shake my head. That wasn't true. Why would she say that? She couldn't see me in the room.

'It was Ian who caused the most damage to Jude. But it was you who covered his face with a cushion and smothered him.'

'You couldn't see me!'

'You told me what had happened. I knew it was an accident, so I said Ian had done it. I wanted to protect you.'

'No.' All the anger of the past thirteen years is coming to a head. My mother's eyes glaze over as she tries to focus. Nausea tears through me and I squeeze my eyes shut for a moment. But all I can see is my ten-year-old self holding Jude in my arms, just as my mother is telling me. I'd wanted to take away his pain. He was suffering. No child should have to live like we did. I'd wanted it to end.

No, she is wrong. I didn't kill him. I couldn't have. I was getting my memories confused, thinking only of what she was telling me. It's my imagination, not what actually happened.

I shake my head. 'You're lying.'

'If anyone saw what you'd done, you'd have been in terrible trouble.'

'You're just saying that to make me feel sorry for you. Ian killed Jude.'

Maria shakes her head too. 'You did.'

'I said no!' I punch her in the stomach. It feels so good, so I hit her again.

Two minutes later, I glance at my handiwork. I'm done with her and her lies now, so I leave her. I need to get cleaned up before I go to see Eva.

But after another shower to rid me of Maria's blood, I take a nap for a couple of hours. Seeing my mother took it out of me, but now I feel ready to face the evening.

*

In the kitchen, I pour a large measure of whisky and knock it back quickly. Then I make Eva's sandwich and add extra sedative to her cup of tea. It's Zopiclone this evening, to make her sleep a little deeper. I wait for it to settle, place it on a tray with the sandwich and head down to the cellar.

'Only me,' I say as I take each step, laughing at my joke. Who else would it be?

'I heard screaming. What's going on?' Eva asks when I open the hatch.

'Relax, it's nothing for you to worry about,' I say, then push through the tray. 'It was something I was watching on the TV.'

CHAPTER SIXTY-TWO

Eva

Eva drank her tea. She wished whatever was in it would make her sleep right now. She didn't care. She just wanted to get another night out of the way. Because those screams were worrying her.

Eva's plan to get close and do as Alex wanted, write her story and then be released, had backfired. It seemed her intervention had made Alex more volatile day by day.

But Alex had a choice, if she could just get through to her. Alex could change from today if she wanted to. There was no point in dwelling on the past, even if you couldn't live with what had happened. And Eva knew of lots of organisations that would help, if only Alex would let someone in.

She thought back to what she'd heard during the day. First it had been the doorbell, then murmurs of conversation.

She'd rushed to her feet. If someone was visiting, she had to let them know she was here.

Eva had screamed, banging her fists on the door. 'Down here. I'm down here.'

But despite her efforts, no one had come to her. And once she heard loud music, she knew Alex had sussed her.

She would be punished later, no doubt, but right then she hadn't cared. She'd had to try and had been dog-tired with the effort, as well as devastated it hadn't worked.

And then she'd slept on and off for a while, until she'd sat up in bed after hearing a scream. She thought it was a spillover from her dream. But then she heard it again. Someone was in a lot of pain. It didn't sound like Alex's voice. Was it Jill? Was she alive?

Eva had gone over to the door again. But after listening to the woman in distress, she'd slid down the wall. Eventually, she'd covered her ears to stop the cries of agony. She couldn't do anything about it while she was here. And she didn't want to think that it was Jill.

And then Alex had turned up with a sandwich and a lukewarm tea. Taking this was okay, but she was starting to worry exponentially about the final drink. After all the lies and storytelling, Eva couldn't be certain that Jill had died from too much of the drug. She wanted her to still be there, alive and locked up in another room, especially after the screams.

Eva had seen a difference in Alex during the past few days. She was going more and more off the rails. She was blaming everyone else for everything. Alex had suffered as a child, and she had lost her brother. But that didn't mean she could do whatever she wanted. Nor did it make it right what she had done so far.

All the women who had been abducted had suffered. No one should be allowed to do that to another human without being punished for it. Anyone could behave like a victim. Eva too, if it weren't for the love she'd received from her aunt and uncle.

So as much as she had pity for Alex, and the numerous children who went off the rails after suffering traumas, not all of them took their troubles into their adult lives. There were umpteen charities set up by victims of abuse who went on to help others, not taking their problems and inflicting them on innocent people.

Because that was what Eva had suspected to be true all along. These women had done nothing to Alex. She was making it all up. Maybe she didn't realise what she was doing, her mind choosing to think otherwise. There could be no other explanation.

Eva could have gone feral after what had happened when she was twelve. She could have had a terrible life too, as well as her brother, but she chose to put the pain behind her. She wouldn't let herself be defined by it.

Instead, she'd picked a career where she could help. Through her articles in the *Stoke News*, she'd been able to make sense of some things and offer justice to people, who were like herself in some ways, wanting to better themselves.

Eva was proud of the work she did. Through it she'd wanted to give the invisible victims, like her mum, a voice – because her own childhood had turned out better than some statistics would have people believe.

Alex could be about to take all that away from her. Eva's life, her voice, her job.

But still something was telling her to fight, to not give up.

DAY 9

21 August 2019

CHAPTER SIXTY-THREE

Alex

I sit by the monitor watching Eva as I sip my coffee. I didn't sleep much last night. I can barely contain my eagerness as I wait for her to wake up.

I'm wondering if Eva's been thinking about what to expect on her final day tomorrow. She certainly doesn't know what's going to happen today. I imagine being kept in a cellar for so long makes a person lose all sense of time. That's why I've given her the newspaper each evening. It seems pointless keeping it from her, because I reckon it intensifies her sense of fear, but also enhances her hope. A double-edged sword. Eva is expecting to go home tomorrow. Her fate is in my hands.

It feels good to be in control again.

By my side is Maria's handbag. I open it and look inside. There is the usual paraphernalia. A packet of handkerchiefs, a set of house keys. A small make-up bag. Underneath them all is a purse. I take it out, unzipping the seal. There's only one note in it, a twenty. A fair bit of shrapnel but no bank cards. My mother did live frugally, it's good to see.

There are pockets so I look through them and find an old photo. It is folded into four. I pull it out and open it up. It's of our family, and I smile. Me and Jude are sitting on a bench, my mum one side. My dad is the other. It's taken at the seaside, on the prom. The sea is in the distance and we're dressed for summer.

We were on holiday for the week, and we'd been out for lunch. Dad insisted we walk and we were tired. I look closer. My face is a picture, really, I seem to be in a strop. Jude is smiling though. He always smiled. I wish I shared his optimism.

Movement on the monitor catches my eye. Ah, let the fun begin.

CHAPTER SIXTY-FOUR

Eva

Eva opened her eyes slowly, her head groggy. Whatever Alex had given her last night to make her sleep had certainly worked better than the previous nights. She worried about the baby and the damage it might do, but equally, needs must at the moment. She had to get through the next two days: fight like never before.

Slowly, she sat up in bed, her aching limbs crying out. She was missing exercise, growing weaker each day without enough nourishment, fresh air and the means to move her muscles.

Then she screamed. There was a woman lying on the floor at the foot of the mattress.

At first she feared it was Jill Bradshaw, but she soon realised the build and hair colour was wrong. And the hair she could see was soaked in blood.

Was she dead?

Eva took in some deep breaths to calm herself, unable to move with fear. She turned back to look at the woman again. What a state she was, naked and covered in bruises.

When had Alex put her in the room? She pushed away a vague thought she may have been alive then and Eva could have helped her.

If Alex had done this, what would she do to her? She was clearly out of control now.

She heard a groan and saw the woman's hand move a little.

Oh, she was alive!

She crawled over to her and kneeled by her side.

With a shaky hand, she touched the woman's shoulder.

'Are you okay?' she asked.

'Alex?' The woman spoke.

'My name is Eva. I won't hurt you, but I don't think I can help you much either.'

The woman flinched as she tried to push herself up to sitting position. Eva helped as best she could. It was then she saw her hair had been chopped at, her nails had been painted black and the tattoo on her neck… She shuddered. There wasn't a number this time. The word 'Judas' had been inked in large letters.

'Rest your back on the wall. I'm sorry but I don't have any water for you to drink. What's your name?'

'Maria Dixon.'

Eva gasped. It was Alex's mum. Was this what had tipped Alex over the edge yesterday, adding to the trauma of the chats they'd had over the past few days? Had that been the catalyst?

'Do you remember how you got here?' she asked.

'I was visiting.' Maria gave out a sob. 'I hurt all over.'

'Alex will have done that to you,' Eva said. 'She's drugged you, just like she did me. You'll get some of your memory back over the next few hours, but you probably won't recall what happened last night.' Eva reached over to the mattress, pulled off the sheet and wrapped it around the woman.

'Thank you.' Maria gave a faint smile. Her head fell to the side a little as she looked at Eva again. 'You're the woman off the news.'

'Yes.'

'Does that mean…?'

She nodded. 'I'm one of five women who have been abducted. By Alex.'

Maria's face creased up. It was a mass of deep purples and ruby reds and there was a cut at her temple. Her hands were swollen too.

'How long have you been here?'

'Nine days.' Eva cleared her throat as her voice came out as a croak. 'What about you?'

'She invited me for lunch yesterday.' Maria coughed a little before continuing. 'We've been in touch for a few months now but it's the first time we've met since… Before that, I thought we were getting along. I should have realised sooner that it wouldn't work.'

'She's mixed up, extremely fragile and equally dangerous, in my opinion. All I want is to go home, but I don't think that will happen.'

Eva got up and went to the door. She banged on it, hoping to get Alex's attention. But even when her hands were burning, she couldn't stop. Eventually though, when it was clear no one would come to them, she dropped her arms.

As Maria's face screwed up in pain, Eva sat by her side. She put an arm around her, careful not to make her move too much. The tang of blood hung in the air, reminding her of the day her mum died. She closed her eyes. She didn't want to see it here too.

She pulled Maria in closer and put a hand to her temple in the hope she could at least offer comfort. It must have been her screams she'd heard yesterday. Alex was getting more dangerous by the day. And even though she was worried for her own safety, Maria would die without help.

She was going to die without help.

Because she wasn't even sure if Alex would still be in the house after what she'd done, or if they were alone.

Trapped where no one would find them.

Maria's head lolled to one side and her eyes closed again. Eva had to keep her talking.

'Tell me about Alex,' she encouraged.

CHAPTER SIXTY-FIVE

Maria

Maria knew there was no way Alex would come to their rescue, and she hadn't seen anyone else helping her in the house. Alex locked her and Eva in there. So when Eva kept asking her questions, she did her best to respond.

'Lara,' she said. 'That's Alex's real name. I'd been so nervous on the way to see her that my legs buckled at one point. I didn't want to take another step. But I pushed on because I needed to see my daughter. See how she had grown up. I wanted to know everything.'

'Had you learned anything about her beforehand?'

'Not really. She was vague in her emails. I couldn't wait to see her but I was anxious too. And yet, now I realise nothing could have changed. I shouldn't have dreamed of a happy reunion. I'm so sorry I wasn't there for her.

'And if we don't get out of here, no one will miss me. It won't hurt me either. Nothing can do that to me any more. I know I've served my sentence for the crime I committed, but I genuinely believe I deserve to die.'

'Don't say that.'

'It's true. I had no right to have children in the first instance.'

'Alex told me a lot of things,' Eva said. 'I'm sure most of them are not true, but she said her dad was the kindest man and that

everything had started to go wrong after his death, and when Ian
came along.'

'That's true. I could barely look after myself let alone two
children. My parents helped for a while, but I knew I had to learn
to survive on my own. I went back home a couple of weeks later.
A few months after that, I met Ian. He pushed himself into my
life and then I couldn't get him out of it.

'I didn't realise he hated my children until he'd sweet talked
his way into our home. Before I knew it, he'd moved in and I was
trapped. His rages were so very frightening. I've often thought how
I would have done things differently had I known what would
happen.' She coughed as pain rushed through her. 'I wasn't able
to help Jude on the night he died. I was in bed. He'd beaten me
that evening. I wasn't even allowed to see my children.'

'I bet it was rough in prison. I imagine being inside for the
murder of a child would be horrific.'

'If I'm being really honest, it was a relief.' Maria pulled a face
and held on to her stomach.

'Are you okay?' Eva asked.

Maria nodded slightly.

'You seem in a lot of pain. I wish I could do something for you.'

'I'm fine,' she fibbed. Really she was wondering what internal
damage Alex might have caused. Something wasn't right.

'I got my comeuppance from the other women when they
found out what I'd done,' Maria continued. 'But at least at night
I was locked in a cell where no one could harm me. I was meek
and a target for bullying, but I was lucky that one woman took
me under her wing. I shared the cell with her. I was terrified to
begin with but we're all nice if our shells are cracked. Well, I like
to think so anyway. She was named Sandra – in for murdering
her abusive husband. *C'est la vie.*

'Sandra saved me. She listened to me and, much more, she
believed me. She looked after me until she was released six years

later. By that time I was able to cope better, having been institutionalised. And far better than how I've been doing on the outside, since, if I'm honest. My parents are both dead now. I have no one. It's horrible being alone.'

'I think it's tragic that you were unable to make amends,' Eva said. 'But I can understand, too, why it never happened.'

'I know I can't expect her forgiveness. I miss my husband, and Jude. Lara too. I've had too much time on my hands to think how I would have done things differently. I've taken the blame for it, all of it. I was controlled and I had no choice, but I should have been stronger. And I thought I might have been able to put things right. That's why I was so excited to be seeing Lara.'

'She's had a tragic life,' Eva admitted. 'If what she's told me is true.'

'I never thought she'd harm me like this.' Maria coughed. 'But then what did I expect after all we'd put her through? Alex was mixed up, damaged and dangerous because of me and Ian. What he did to my children was cruel, heartless and unforgiving. No one knows the real truth. I was so scared of him. I never dared to stand up to him for fear of what he might do. He would come home paralytic and take it out on me in the evenings, and the kids had to be quiet during the day or else he'd have a go at them too. I barely got out of bed some mornings because of the pain he'd exert on me the night before. Often I wish I hadn't woken up at all.'

'It must have been unbearable,' Eva soothed.

'He told me he didn't love me many times, and that he wouldn't leave until he had somewhere to go. I thought about telling the police but I was too scared. I'd only known a relationship like my marriage. Ian was different to anyone I knew. I was stupid enough to fall for his charms and then I couldn't get rid of him. It's funny, but I was planning on leaving that weekend and getting away with the twins.'

'You might not believe me but I do understand why you stayed.' Eva sniffed. 'My mum was a victim of domestic abuse. She was too scared to leave.'

'Did she get away?'

When Eva didn't reply, Maria thought the worst must have happened.

'My children… they didn't deserve what they got,' she said. 'Especially Jude. He was such a sweet boy. Lara was a lovely girl back then too. How it changed her was my fault. They both suffered so much. I-I tried to help. I used to give them food when he'd said they couldn't have any. But then he got wind of it, and so whenever he came in, he'd ask them if I'd given them anything. They always said no, but he knew when they were lying. Well, what was I to do? I was terrified. I knew what he was capable of.'

Suddenly a rush of warmth in her stomach made her groan in agony. It was as if someone had taken the stop out of a water bottle. She could feel liquid sloshing around in her abdomen.

She gasped, holding on to Eva's hand as the pain got much worse.

CHAPTER SIXTY-SIX

Eva

Eva struggled with her emotions the whole while Maria talked.

'She has shared some of that with me for the story I'm writing for her,' she told Maria, 'but I'm struggling to distinguish the truth from the lies. She seems so damaged by it all.'

As Maria groaned again, Eva pulled her closer. She held in a sob. What else could she do but comfort her and hope to talk some sense into Alex when she next saw her? Maria needed to see a doctor.

It had been hours since she'd heard anything upstairs though. And the thoughts running through her head at the moment weren't pleasant. Had Alex gone? Had she left them both to die in there? Would she have killed herself after what she'd done to her mum? Was the game over for them both?

She shuddered. Stop it, she told herself.

'I'm really sorry for what happened to my children.' Maria's voice was a whisper. 'Ian locked them up in the room overnight, and I didn't dare go in. But Ian hadn't told me what he'd done, that Jude was badly injured. Had he done, Jude might have survived. But he's gone and I can't do any more for Lara now. She needs to face her demons before she gets better.'

Eva couldn't ever imagine that happening.

'I'm tired,' Maria whispered. 'I want to go to sleep.'

'You rest now.' Eva stroked Maria's head. Her pallor was nearly as grey as her hair, fading by the minute. There was nothing more Eva could do. Maria was dying and Alex didn't want to know.

'I'm going to get you for this, Alex,' Eva whispered.

As Maria's breathing slowed and then finally stopped, Eva sat quietly crying. She felt so helpless, useless even.

But then a pain shot through her stomach, causing her to wince. A cramp like a period pain. Struggling to breathe through the discomfort, she rested her hand on her stomach before it came again, and she drew up her knees.

Please no, she sobbed into the room.

With the stress of the situation, she knew her baby was dying too.

*

Eva wasn't sure how long she sat with Maria after she died. She didn't want to move her, or herself. And what would Alex do when she found out she'd killed her own mother? She might go completely off the rails, and where would that leave Eva?

Finally able to face it, she lay Maria out on the floor and covered her with the sheet. She couldn't bear to see her face, dead eyes staring back at her, knowing she was unable to help her.

Distress made her weep. Maria had met the wrong man on the rebound after her husband had died and, even though it was her home, was too scared to leave him. Just like Eva's mum with her dad.

Eva's stomach cramps were still happening. The despair at losing the life inside her was too much. Now the little hope she was depending on to get her through to the end of this ordeal had been stripped away. Her clothes were speckled with her blood. She'd lost the will to think of her own survival.

So if Alex was still there, she would take the drink that evening. She'd had enough.

*

It was hours before Alex finally showed up. Eva had had no food or drink since the night before, so she laughed with relief when she heard the door to the cellar opening. The hatch was opened and a tray pushed through. Next to her usual sandwich and cup of tea was a bottle of water. She picked up the food instead.

'Your mother is dead,' she told Alex as she bit greedily into it.

'I know. I've been watching you on the monitor. I had thought I might feel something but I don't.' Alex paused. 'Do you think that's strange?'

Eva thought it was sick but refrained from shouting it out. She didn't owe Alex conversation any more. Not after what she'd done to Maria, and how she had left her to deal with the mess.

'That's your final drink,' Alex said. 'In the water.'

Eva stared at the bottle in despair. She couldn't even touch it. 'What's it to be?'

'I don't know what to do,' she replied.

'Drink it and find out where you are when you wake up.'

'If I wake up.'

Alex's laughter was cruel and taunting. 'Well, there is that. But I have been careful with the dosage this time.'

'And if I don't take the drink?'

'Then you'll never know if I'm going to free you.'

It was a heartbreaking decision to make, but she had to drink it if she wanted to get out and go home. Even if there weren't enough drugs in the drink to kill her, she was certain she didn't want to wake up in the room and not be able to see Nick again. Alex was remorseless. She might want Eva to stay in the cellar until she died.

Yet what state would she be in if she did wake up? Look what Alex had done to Maria. What would she do to her?

Eva pulled at her blonde hair, perhaps for the last time. She looked at her nails: dirty with varnish peeling off. The clothes she had on stank and were stained so she wouldn't be sorry to lose them. But she didn't want to be dumped anywhere naked. She might not even get through the night.

Her baby might not have survived at all.

What should she do?

What would you do, Nick? Please help me to decide.

'Eva, what's it to be?' Alex's voice had an impatient strain to it.

'I don't know,' she whispered.

'Yes, you do. It will all be over if you take the drink.'

'I can't.'

'You can.'

'No, I—'

'If I have to come in there and force it down you, I will!'

With tears pouring down her face, Eva reached for the water. Before she could think any more about the consequences, she drank it back as quickly as possible. If Alex was thinking of killing her anyway, then this might be the best way to go.

CHAPTER SIXTY-SEVEN

Alex

I thought I'd feel something when Eva told me my mother was dead. All the years I've wanted to take my revenge, planning to harm her when I did see her, have come to fruition.

It happened a little earlier than I'd intended. The original idea was to tie her to a chair and kill her in front of Eva, before I let Eva go. The drugs I would have administered to Eva meant she perhaps might not remember any of it, but I would. And I would have had the memory to treasure forever. But it wasn't meant to be. Never mind.

I honestly wasn't sure if Eva would drink the water I gave to her, after I'd mentioned what had happened to Jillian. Part of me thinks she's a gullible bitch for doing so. The other part of me thinks good on her. She's weak, she's scared and she doesn't want to die. But nor does she want to be imprisoned in that room for a minute longer.

I wonder if she's thinking about Nick. He's been in the news a lot this week, talking about his wife and how much he loves her. He says he has faith that she will come home soon, broken, but alive and that he can repair any damage I've done. I really did laugh out loud at that. Who does he think he is – superman? Eva will be impossible to restore once I've finished with her. She may never write again.

Actually, that's a good idea. Perhaps I should cut her fingers off so she can't type.

I laugh now too. I may be heartless, but I will always take the easy way out of things. I couldn't cut off limbs. I'm not one of those weirdos who hide different body parts everywhere so as not to get caught. I don't kill for fun. It's not premeditated. I just do it when I lose control, or things aren't going my way. It happens, and I'm not going to apologise for it.

Enough sitting around. I need to pack my bag. I want to be ready to leave as quickly as possible tomorrow once everything is over. But first, I have to do one more thing.

I reach for the card I have bought for Milly. It has an illustration of a little bear holding hands with a small girl, walking off into the sunset together. I take a piece of paper and write a note in my best handwriting:

Dearest Milly

I just wanted to say thank you for being my friend over these past months. I've enjoyed our time together so much and it has been a pleasure getting to know you. I've loved reading and discussing books with you and I will miss that in the future. Because once you get this letter, you will know I can't see you any more.

You might hear stuff about me in the news but please don't believe it all. I needed to do some things before I left. I had a plan, you see. Meeting you wasn't part of it but it was wonderful to have your friendship along the way. You made things much easier for me and I always looked forward to our weekly meetups.

All I ask now is that you continue to do well at school, get good grades and the best education you can and make something of yourself. Don't be like me, so wound up on getting revenge that it ruined the life I could have had.

I'm sure you'll make new friends soon. But for now, I've left you a pile of books in the shed. I know you'll enjoy reading them, even if you don't have someone like me to talk to about them.

Who knows, one day, you might pick up a message from me. I would love to hear how you are doing. But for now, I need to stay low. I hope you understand.

I will miss you so much!

Lots of love, Alex x

DAY 10

22 August 2019

CHAPTER SIXTY-EIGHT

Eva

Eva groaned as an ache sliced across her forehead. She pressed a hand to it as she tried to sit up. At least the room seemed dark; she had a feeling that any light would be torture.

She flinched as pain erupted in her stomach. She sat up further and she steadied herself on the wall with a hand. Her head was banging but that seemed to be all.

What the…?

Tears pricked her eyes. She was still in the cellar. Wasn't the plan to get out of there last night? It had been day nine, and she'd had to take the drink to escape. She'd obviously been compliant by drinking it, as she didn't seem to have many injuries.

But why was she still in the room? What was Alex's plan now?

She swivelled her legs until her feet were on the floor. She put a hand up to her hair, laughing in relief to find it was all there. She splayed out her fingers. Her nails hadn't been touched, and there was no warm feeling on her neck where she might have had a tattoo. Hopefully, she hadn't been left with a reminder.

Except for Maria.

She turned to her left a little more. Maria was still in the corner of the room. How had she slept last night with a dead body near to her? Eva had assumed Alex would have come into the room to remove it. Although, the drugs in the water didn't seem to have had the same effect on her as it had ten days ago. Was that because Alex was being careful after what had happened to Jill, or hadn't she wanted to give Eva too much for another reason? Or perhaps she'd been given a milder sedative.

Because she was still here in the cellar, and it was day ten.

She wept.

She'd wanted to be outside so much, on her way home. Despite her wobbles, she had rested all her hope on that. Now it had been dashed and an overwhelming feeling of doom crashed down on her.

Which is why it took a while for her to see that the cellar door wasn't closed any more. It was ajar.

She stood up slowly, hoping she could walk. She marched on the spot for a few seconds, waving her arms round like a windmill to get a little feeling back. Most of her body seemed okay. She had a raging headache though – caused by the drugs or Alex, she wasn't sure. She put her hands out in front – they were shaking but they were okay. No bruises.

Dizziness washed over her and she sat on the mattress again.

Why was the door open? It must be a trick. Surely Alex wouldn't let her roam the house after being captive all this time? When she would try to escape no matter what.

Because that was her first thought now.

Was Alex waiting for her to come out of the room? Why hadn't she taken her to be found somewhere? Despair tore through her as she realised she might not be going home after all.

She listened. Silence. Would Alex have left the door open purposely? Or had she forgotten to close it? Was Alex in the house or had she left for the day?

So many questions.

After a few minutes, she stood up again, feeling a little steadier. Unsure what she would be facing, she walked towards the door.

She pushed it open and saw the steps ahead of her. She looked around but could see nothing she could use to defend herself.

She walked slowly towards them and went up carefully, not a thought to what might be underfoot on her bare skin.

There was a door at the top of those steps. After a deep breath, she pressed down the handle.

CHAPTER SIXTY-NINE

Eva

Eva found herself in a kitchen. It was a large square with a small pine table in the middle of it. A mug was atop of it. Eva put her hand to it. It was cold.

She made her way slowly across the floor. The tiles were icy on her feet and she shivered, hugging herself for comfort.

She opened the fridge door to see what food there was. She dived on a small block of cheese, and fresh slices of ham, cramming them into her mouth. There was bottled water in the door, but she left them, unsure they hadn't been tampered with. Instead, she turned on the cold water tap as quietly as she could and drank straight from there.

The house was deathly silent but she didn't doubt for a moment that she was alone. Alex wouldn't have left the door open by mistake. Not after all her meticulous planning. Unless she had taken drugs too.

The thought made her heart race. Perhaps she was on her own now. She moved towards the back door, disappointed but expectant when she found it locked. There was no key nearby she could see. She would have to try the front door.

Before she did, she opened a few cupboards. Spotting a packet of biscuits, she ripped them open and crammed one in her mouth.

She kept a couple in her hands, eating as she moved around. She opened a drawer to find cutlery, rooting out a small knife. She tucked it up her sleeve, the cuff on the sweatshirt keeping it in place.

She tiptoed across the tiles. The other door leading from the kitchen was shut and again she pushed down a handle, grimacing as the sound seemed to reverberate around the room. It opened with a groan, and she waited for a second or two to see if anyone would appear.

She could see a hallway in front of her. A door to her right was closed. Stairs above her to her left. There was nowhere for anyone to hide.

No sound from anywhere.

Ahead of her was the front door. If she could get through it, she was free. If only it were that simple. She knew the logics of every scary movie she'd watched with Nick. Alex could be lying in wait in the shadows for her, hoping to creep out at the optimum time. But how would she have known she would appear upstairs at that exact moment?

She stepped forward, taking tiny steps to make the least amount of noise. She couldn't hear a TV or radio. The house was silent, except for her breathing.

She got to the bottom of the stairs and stopped. There was another door to her left, with a further room off it. That door was open. Eva could see part of an armchair and a large window, cream carpeting and curtains. She turned to look up the stairs, half-expecting to see Alex standing at the top with a poker ready to launch at her.

Heart racing, she took the final steps to the front door. She pushed the handle, only to find it locked with no key she could put her hand to.

Tears of frustration fell, her shoulders dropping. All the easy exits were blocked. There was no way out, unless she checked in the other rooms.

She tried the room with the door open first, pushing on it tentatively. There was a dining table. In front of one of the chairs was a laptop, a vase of flowers, a box of chocolates and a bottle of wine.

Her notepad sat on top of the laptop, but she merely glanced at it. Instead she looked at the window. It was a bay, two smaller panes of glass either side of a large one. It was single-paned. She could get through it if she broke the glass. But she didn't dare to bring attention to herself yet. Not until she knew she was alone.

Outside, there was a small garden, a drop to a lawned area and a narrow driveway. A wall stood at the end of it, about three feet high. And then a road. To freedom. There didn't seem to be anyone around though.

She pulled at the catches on the handles but both were locked. Eva knew she kept her own window keys in the most bizarre places. She scanned the room, looking behind a pile of travel magazines, a photo frame on a side unit, inside a drawer.

'Looking for anything in particular?' A voice came from behind her.

And just like that all of Eva's hopes of getting out of there evaporated. Pinpricks erupted all over her skin and she had to stop from shouting out.

It was a weird feeling: she wanted to see who it was but dreaded it too.

Who had harmed her, tortured her, almost starved her and mentally drained her?

Slowly she turned to see who had held her captive for ten days.

Eva inhaled. Of course, Alex had told her she wouldn't use her own name, but still. She hadn't expected the woman to be someone she knew.

'Jessica?' she said.

CHAPTER SEVENTY

Eva

Eva stood dumbfounded, the woman in front of her holding a carving knife down to her side.

'Oh, so you do know my name!' Alex cried.

'Of course. But I don't understand.'

'You really didn't know?' Alex moved towards her. 'I gave you lots of clues and you're married to a police officer, so you'd have access to inside information too.'

Eva's head was fuzzy as she tried to work everything out. As Jessica, Alex had worked for the *Stoke News*. She was on the IT Helpdesk and had often come to assist her when her computer had been down, or her laptop wasn't working.

'Why would—'

'I've been watching you for some time. It pleased me that you stayed in the one place for so long. It was easy for me to keep a tab on you. You journalists and your bylines. You're everywhere online – I can find you in a moment.'

'You've been working at the newspaper to get to me?'

'Not exactly. But you played a big part in my plan. I had to bide my time to find a job there. I applied for every vacancy I could over a year before an opening for an IT technician came up. Technology fascinates me, but I would have filed or answered the phone all day to get close to you.' She threw a thumb over her shoulder. 'I taught myself how to hack a phone and a hard drive. It was so easy to blend in the background, get close to you and yet you had no idea.'

Eva wasn't sure she was capable of speaking. But Alex continued regardless.

'I got into your computer. I have all your emails, all the reports on the missing women. I cancelled your meeting with David Wood ten days ago, and then I deleted the email once he'd replied. Although luckily for him, he was able to prove it existed so he wasn't questioned by the police for long.'

Eva's brain was foggy due to the medication, so she couldn't work things out quickly enough. At work she had felt sorry for Alex. As Jessica, Alex had seemed a quiet soul, like a mouse. They had hardly any conversations, no matter how many times Eva had tried to include her. It was as if she wanted to live on the periphery. In the end, she'd put it down to her being an introvert and had stopped badgering her to join in for fear of offending her.

Except over the past few weeks.

Alex had really homed in on Eva, talking to her and going out of her way to be with her on her breaks. Now it all made sense.

'How – how did I get here?' Eva asked.

'I rang you in distress and you came to see me straight away. I then drove your car to a secluded spot so it could be found. You're such a caring person coming to see me. For that, I was going to release you at the end of the ten days, until you grabbed my arm and forced me to talk to you. Then I realised how I could use you to write my story. Although now you know, there might not be a happy ending after meeting my mother.'

Eva was having a hard time listening to what she was saying, never mind trying to work everything out. Her head was banging. She put a hand to her stomach, hoping to shield her baby. Hoping that they would both survive whatever was going to happen next. Then her heart sank when she realised there was nothing.

That was Alex's fault.

'You let me down, just like all the other women,' Alex went on. 'You reported on me in court, making everyone feel sorry for me. But it was after your words were written that you stopped caring.'

'That's not true.'

'So what day is it today?'

'I don't know.'

'It's my birthday, and that's why it's day ten for you.'

Eva understood then. It would have been Jude's birthday too.

'Have you any idea what it's like, unable to celebrate because the other half of you is dead? I don't feel complete without Jude. I miss him so much. And you? You could have helped me all those years ago. And you did nothing!'

'I don't know what you mean.'

'You really don't remember, do you?'

Eva shook her head.

'In court, you spoke to me when I went to the bathroom. You said everything would be fine, but it wasn't, was it?'

2007

CHAPTER SEVENTY-ONE

Eva

Eva had been chatting to her editor in court when she noticed the little girl slip into the ladies'. Excusing herself, she followed her.

Inside, she found her sitting on a chair, her tiny legs going back and forth as she couldn't reach the floor. She seemed so small, and yet she had been through so much at such a young age.

'Are you okay?' Eva asked her, knowing that she might not get a chance to speak to her again.

The girl nodded.

'You were very brave in court,' she added. 'That was you, wasn't it?' She raised a hand when she saw the girl look at the door and her face drop. 'Don't worry, I won't say anything to anyone. I just wanted to say well done. It can't have been nice to sit through all this, not after what happened to you and your brother.'

The girl didn't speak.

Eva wondered now why she'd followed her. It wasn't ethical to talk to her, but she hadn't done it for that reason. The girl looked lost, and she'd wanted to reassure her that things would get better.

'When I was twelve, my dad killed my mum,' she said. 'I don't think he meant to, but he did, and my life changed forever on that day. I went to live with my aunt and uncle and, although it wasn't the same, and I'll never forget my mum, things turned out okay in the end.' Eva smiled. 'Change isn't easy, especially when you're grieving, but when you grow up, you can do anything you want. You can be anything you want. You need to look after yourself, do well at school and make everyone proud. I think you're capable of that. You seem very bright to me.' She nudged her playfully. 'Don't you think?'

There was a small smile and a quick glance in her direction, but nothing else. Eva got up and headed for a cubicle. As she was about to close the door, she heard a voice.

'What's going to happen to me?'

'I don't know, sweetheart. But someone will look after you.'

The door to the corridor opened, and Eva rushed into a cubicle before she could be seen.

'There you are,' she heard a woman say. 'We've got to go now. Come along.'

'Can I have an ice cream, please?' The door opened.

'Of course you can. What would you like?'

Eva didn't hear the reply as the door closed again. But she didn't stop thinking about Witness 1575.

What a start in life that child would have. A mother in prison. A brother who was killed by someone who wasn't related to them. A child now in the hands of the local authorities until she was sixteen.

All because of one evil bastard.

DAY 10

22 August 2019

CHAPTER SEVENTY-TWO

Eva

Eva couldn't see a way out of this now. What did Alex mean, saying she hadn't done anything for her? Eva was a journalist, not a support worker. Had Alex latched on to the idea that she should have helped her when she was a child?

Of course now Eva remembered their meeting in court, she'd thought she was giving a little girl some encouragement, just like the other women Alex had abducted.

And that's how Alex had known about her parents. Eva had told her some of her past. Just a few lines of dialogue carried through the years to hunt her down.

She decided to plead with Alex.

'I'm sorry,' she said. 'I wanted to give you some hope.'

Alex laughed. 'That went well, didn't it? Look at me now.'

'It doesn't have to be like this.'

'No, it doesn't. If it weren't for you, I'd be out of here by now. I have a bag packed, tickets booked on a plane tonight. But now I need to get things finished, tie things up.' Alex pointed to the laptop at the other end of the table. 'I want you to type up your notes. How you behave towards me today will decide your future.' Alex smiled sweetly. 'It's such a good game, don't you think?'

Eva nodded, unsure if the question needed answering but doing so anyway. She ran a tongue around her dry mouth and swallowed.

Alex pointed to the chair. 'Sit down.'

Eva moved towards the table. Alex pulled out a chair and picked up a roll of duct tape from its seat.

'I want you to bind your legs to the chair. Do it!' Alex shouted.

Eva flinched, but took the roll from her and did as she'd been told.

'That's better.' Alex slid the laptop towards her and opened it.

As the screen came to life, Eva could see it was set up on a blank document.

Alex sat in the armchair and rested the knife in her lap. 'Right, get typing,' she said.

Eva began, only then noticing the wine was a Merlot, the flowers were lilies, and the chocolates were pure cocoa. All things she'd told Alex she liked during their conversations. Was she trying to tease her?

She wasn't waiting to find out. She was going to play this by the book and get out of here.

She had to get out of here.

Because Maria Dixon dying in her arms had changed every-thing.

CHAPTER SEVENTY-THREE

Eva

Eva typed away at the notes in the book. She estimated it would take her at least three hours to get everything written out. All the while, Alex made polite talk as if they were friends meeting in a café.

'Do you know how easy it is to find out where people live?' Alex said. 'People think it's hard, but it isn't. You see, no one's really watching. They're too busy on their phones, rushing around, not paying attention.' She laughed. 'I just followed you home. It was that simple.'

Eva remained poker-faced when all she wanted to do was scream, hit out and run.

'I did the same with the other women too. I've been stalking you all on and off for over a year.'

'How did you get everyone here?' Eva had to ask, she was so curious to know. 'It must have been hard not to be seen.'

'Not when you drug people. I used Rohypnol, but then I assume you might have guessed that. I read your feature on it. It was good – gave me some advice.' Alex pulled her feet up beside her on the chair. 'I followed Stephanie, and once she was out of her car, I introduced myself. She was pleased to see me, and I suggested we go for a coffee. She's such a gullible cow. I didn't even have to cajole her. While she slipped to the loo, I added the liquid in the drink and then, when she started to feel woozy, I acted as if I was taking her home. By the time we got here, she was easy to manipulate. I told her she could rest in the cellar.'

Alex's smirk was unnerving but Eva remained calm.

'After that it was easy. I did the same to the others. I spoke to Maxine when she was in town waiting for a friend – that would be me after I'd emailed her from someone else's account. I hacked into that too. Then I introduced myself to Alison.

'Jillian was a bit harder to get close to, but I reported a prowler in my garden and she was sent to see me. It was amazing how out of all the police officers, she turned up on my doorstep!'

Eva said nothing. Jill wasn't who Alex had thought she was. It could have been any woman officer who called and they would have been kidnapped.

'And now you're here, to tell my story and complete my plan. I've waited for this moment for so long. It's poetic, don't you think? The killer daughter and the journalist. It has such a good ring to it.'

At the mention of killer, Eva recoiled.

'All that computer stuff I learned came in handy,' Alex sniggered. 'I changed my name. Identity fraud. Alex is the name of a woman who died when she was thirty-two. I have her details cloned.'

'Your mum told me your real name was Lara.'

'My name is Alex. But I can use whichever you prefer.'

Eva's head was fit to burst with the information Alex had given her over the past hour. She didn't know what to think. Instead she kept her mind on typing up the notes and imagining herself at home that night with Nick. She knew it was highly unlikely to happen, but still she thought about it.

As well as the knife she had hidden, she eyed up the things in the room she could use as a weapon. There wasn't much: the laptop, the vase, the wine bottle and a framed photo on the sideboard. These were all capable of injuring someone but not stopping them long enough for her to make her escape. And Alex had a knife too, and she wasn't afraid to use it.

Right now, Eva wondered if Alex was completely mad or really smart. Trying to trick her into thinking she would slip up when she would do nothing of the sort.

A shadow caught Eva's eye. Someone walked in front of the window.

'Who was that?' Alex wanted to know.

'I didn't see.'

There was a knock on the door.

'Shit!' Alex stood up and went to the window. She sighed drastically and then held up the knife. 'No funny business while I get rid of her. Do you hear?'

Eva nodded. Even with the knife hidden in her sleeve, there was no chance of her trying to get away now she was bound to the chair. It was too risky, and she'd have to get past Alex. So she waited it out.

But then she heard the front door close and Alex still talking.

Someone had come into the house.

CHAPTER SEVENTY-FOUR

Alex

I curse under my breath for getting too close to Milly. I should never have made friends with anyone. This could ruin my plan completely.

I go to answer the door, hiding the knife out of sight.

'Milly!' I say. 'I wasn't expecting you. Is something wrong?'

Milly holds up a bag. 'I bought you some books. They were on sale – three for five pounds – so I thought we could share.'

'I don't have time to read at the moment!'

Milly jumps at my raised voice.

'Oh! I thought… I thought it would be a nice surprise.'

'But you should have told me you were coming. I'm busy.'

Milly's bottom lip trembles. 'I'm sorry. I—'

There's a noise from the front room. Milly hears it too. In a split second, I beckon her in.

'Come on then, before I change my mind.'

Milly smiles. She's so sweet but I want to wipe it off her face. In fact…

'Go through to the living room,' I tell her, following behind. I almost bump into her as she stops in her tracks when she spots Eva. She turns to me with a look of confusion.

'Give me your phone,' I say, holding out my hand. When she doesn't move, I scream at her. 'Give me your fucking phone!'

Milly obliges then. I tuck it into the pocket of my jeans. Then I draw my hand back and strike her across the face. The force of it sends her crashing to the floor.

'What was that for?' She holds her cheek, already reddening. Her eyes are brimming with tears.

'Get over there,' I demand, pointing to a chair at the table. 'You've given me no alternative now.'

Milly whimpers but moves quickly. I see her glance at Eva, but she says nothing. I reach for the duct tape and quickly wrap it around her ankles, binding her to the chair. Then I fasten her hands together in front of her. She rests them in her lap, unable to say a word. The look of fear on her face stops me from putting tape across her mouth for a moment. Then I rip a piece off and stick it on anyway.

'Right then, a slight change of plan. Eva, meet Milly. Milly, this is Eva. But you already know that, don't you? You must have seen her on the news.'

Milly looks at me and gives a quick nod of her head.

I turn to Eva. 'I'm going to leave you two for a couple of minutes, but I'm warning you, there are cameras in every room and there is a monitor in the kitchen, so I can see what you're up to. No silly games, now.'

It is Eva's turn to nod.

I clap my hands. This might work out better than I'd planned. 'Right then. Who's up for a cup of tea?'

CHAPTER SEVENTY-FIVE

Milly

Milly had recognised the woman sitting at the table in an instant. She'd seen her on the TV only that morning. The police had been looking for her, and she'd been on every bulletin for the past ten days. But everyone was saying it was a man who had kidnapped them.

Surely Alex hadn't kept her here – kept all those women locked up? Milly had been to tea last week, since Eva Farmer had gone missing. It didn't make sense. Had Eva been there all along?

As soon as Alex disappeared, Eva began to speak in a whispered tone.

'I don't have much time to explain, but I've been held captive by Alex, downstairs, in her cellar, for the past ten days. We need to get away from here as soon as we can, but I have to figure out how.'

Milly nodded. She wished she hadn't got the tape across her mouth. She was finding it hard to breathe, trying not to panic.

'I know you're scared but please, stay calm,' Eva told her. 'I'm very weak, as I haven't been given much food, so you'll have to help me. As soon as I ask you something, will you do it for me?'

Milly nodded again. She would do anything to get out of here.

As Eva went back to her typing, Milly sat in a daze. What was going on? All this time she had been friends with Alex, visiting her here, she was abducting women? Torturing them, holding them against their will? It didn't seem like the Alex she knew.

But then again, Alex had just struck her across the face and she hadn't expected that either.

Before she had time to think any more, Alex was back. She came into the room carrying three mugs in one hand, the liquid spilling over the rim, and a packet of biscuits in the other.

As Alex walked towards her, Milly moved back in her chair, pulling her head away.

'Don't be silly, Milly.' Alex laughed. 'How can you drink with that tape over your mouth? If I remove it, you promise not to make a sound?'

Milly nodded.

'Lovely.' Alex bent slightly to put the mugs on the table. She pushed one over to Eva, then put one in front of Milly and the other she moved to the end of the table to a spare chair. Next she pulled the tape from Milly's lips, taking no care at all.

Tears stung Milly's eyes, the skin at the corner of her mouth splitting. She ran a tongue over it as Alex sat down at the end of the table.

'No funny business, ladies.' Alex smiled again. 'We're going to share some time together, like friends do. Right?'

CHAPTER SEVENTY-SIX

Alex

I look at Eva and think about how it all went wrong because of her. All the pent-up feelings I had bottled up were now on display and, even if I say so myself, I'm a little worried about my actions. I never intended to harm Milly. She is my friend.

I look at Milly, fear in her eyes as she sips at her drink, trying not to spill it. Of course, I'm not going to remove the tape from her hands, but I'm not sure what I'm going to do with her now that's she turned up unannounced. I'll have enough trouble getting rid of Eva. What on earth am I going to do with two of them?

Perhaps I should leave them here and make my escape. I still intend on catching my flight this evening. Once I'm at the airport, I'll ring the police and leave an anonymous message to say I've heard noises in the cellar next door.

I'm not cruel enough to leave them to die. Not unless they cross me.

'How are you doing with the words, Eva?' I ask as I sip my drink. 'Got long to go now?'

Eva leafs through the remaining pages she needs to finish. 'I think another hour or so should do it.'

'Great. What can we talk about in the meantime?' I turn to Milly. 'Have you finished the book yet?'

'No,' Milly says.

Her voice has a little quiver, and I laugh and turn to Eva. 'Milly and I have our own book club. We meet once a week, read a book and then discuss it. There's been some great conversations, hasn't there, Mils?'

Milly nods.

'At least you don't have to worry about Jaimie any more.' I clap my hands and grin. 'It was me who sorted her out.'

Milly's eyes widen, and I laugh again. Confessing is so much fun.

'Yes, that's right. I followed her home that night and threatened her. You should be thanking me.' I stop talking and glare at Milly. 'Well?'

'Th-thank you.'

'You're lucky the bullying stopped. You've never had it so good, has she, Eva?' I point at Eva and then at myself. 'We know what it's like to have terrible childhoods: things happening that made everything worse for us. But you don't hear us complaining.' I glare at Milly.

Milly's eyes flick between me and Eva. I wonder if she is shocked at what I've told her. 'Now that Jaimie's out of the picture, you have the chance to settle down and make friends. Get some good grades at school and make a life for yourself. Honestly, I wouldn't wish mine on anyone. It hasn't been enjoyable.'

Milly says nothing.

'Still, I get the chance to start again tomorrow. Somewhere no one knows me. Somewhere I can reinvent myself. Be whoever I want to be. I'll have to think of another name once I'm off the plane. Grab a new identity. Hey, maybe I'll become an Eva, or a Milly. That would be funny, wouldn't it?'

CHAPTER SEVENTY-SEVEN

Eva

It had been three hours since Eva had started typing the remainder of the notes, but she was almost done. All the time she'd been thinking of how she would escape. There were so little options right now.

Alex was still sitting at the head of the table, chatting to them as if nothing odd was happening.

It was hopeless. Unless she could do something simple, so obvious that it might work. Should she fake an illness? No, Alex would see through that.

She started to write in the notepad, crossing through pages as she worked out how much left she had to do. Then she stopped. Could it be that simple?

She put down the pad, knocking her mug over purposely. The liquid spilled across the table, splashing over the keyboard of the laptop.

'You dozy cow!' Alex rolled her eyes as she stepped across the room.

'Sorry.' Eva picked up the pad as if she was trying to salvage it.

'I'll get a cloth. No funny business,' Alex said.

Eva glanced at Milly from the corner of her eye. On her reckoning they had about a minute to remove the tapes, starting with Milly's hands.

As soon as she was out of sight, Eva pressed a finger to her lips and then slipped the knife from out of her sleeve. She reached across and sliced at the tape around Milly's wrists until they were free.

'Untie your feet, quickly,' she whispered.

She bent down to cut through her tape, trying to ignore the noise they were making. She had to get to the door before Alex came back. Once free, she glanced at Milly, who was now standing up. She popped the knife back into her sleeve again.

'Quickly.' She beckoned her over to the sideboard. 'Help me get this in front of the door. We may not have much time.'

They pushed the unit in place, just as the door handle went down on the other side. The women glanced at each other.

'Hey!' Alex banged on the door. 'Let me in, you bitches. What's going on in there?'

Eva grabbed the nearest chair and raised it in the air. 'We have to break the window and climb out. Put a hand on the side of the seat and hold on to the back too.'

Milly came across to her. The banging continued behind them. It would only be a matter of time before Alex pushed the sideboard out of the way enough to squeeze through.

They ran at the window with all their might, four chair legs crashing through the large pane of glass. The deafening sound of a million particles falling to the floor made them freeze.

For a second the banging stopped behind them, but there was no time to look. Eva knew if they weren't quick, Alex would be able to unlock the front door before they had time to clamber through the window, and there was broken glass to contend with.

She poked out what she could with the chair legs. Then she grabbed a cushion from the armchair. She placed it on the window frame to stop them from injuring themselves as Alex continued to push at the door with her shoulder.

Eva could hear the unit sliding across the floor. Any minute now, Alex would be able to squeeze through the gap.

'You first, Milly,' she said. 'When you get outside, run! Near to people and houses. Stop anyone who'll help you, and call the police.'

Milly scrambled through, being careful to miss the jagged glass. Eva held the cushion to stop it from falling and watched as Milly jumped down to the ground.

Alex burst into the room.

'Go, Milly,' Eva encouraged.

'I'm not leaving you.'

From behind them came a cry like a wounded animal.

'Go!'

Eva was relieved to see the young girl running away as Alex climbed over the unit and flew at her. She put one leg over the windowsill.

'You're not getting away!' Alex caught hold of her arm and pulled.

'Let go of me,' Eva cried, curling her fingers into a fist and punching out at Alex's hands.

'You're not going anywhere,' Alex screamed.

Eva had heard people say that even at their lowest ebb, some strength had come to them. She was exhausted, hungry and weak, but fuelled with adrenaline as she fought for her life. If Alex got her back inside the house, she would kill her.

Struggling not to lose her balance, she shrugged the knife from out of the sleeve and into her fist. Then she turned towards Alex. She glared at her before raising the knife in the air and bringing it down into the back of Alex's hand.

Alex let go, and Eva cried out as she fell. The smell of grass invaded her senses. As she looked behind her, Alex stood in the window shouting obscenities. Then Milly was by her side, helping her to her feet. They held on to each other as they ran out of the drive and into the street.

It seemed like forever until they could see someone ahead of them: a man getting into a car. He was waving to a woman on the doorstep at the house he had just left.

'I've found Eva Farmer, the kidnapped journalist,' Milly cried out to him. 'We need the police. Help!'

As the couple rushed towards them, Eva glanced over her shoulder to see if they were alone. Alex was nowhere to be seen.

CHAPTER SEVENTY-EIGHT

Eva

Eva was thankful that Milly was still holding on to her as her legs were so weak. She rested on the wall while the man contacted the emergency services.

'Please come inside,' the woman said to them. 'I'm Rebecca, and that's my husband, Markus. You're safe with us, I promise.'

Helped by them both, Eva was shown into a kitchen at the back of the house. She was placed onto a small settee.

Once she sat down, it was as if the whole burden was lifted from her shoulders, and she burst into tears. It took her a few minutes before she was able to speak.

'Thank you,' she said to Rebecca. 'I feel like we've invaded your home.'

'It's fine.' Rebecca sat next to her and placed her hands over Eva's. 'You can stay here as long as you need to. I'm so pleased you've been found. Everyone has been looking for you. I can't believe you were right under our noses all the time. I'm so sorry we didn't know.'

Eva hadn't mentioned anything about what had happened. She knew it would be best kept until the police arrived. She sat up suddenly. 'Could I use your phone, please?'

'Yes, of course.' Rebecca went to fetch it from the worktop and handed it to her. 'Would you like to be left alone?'

Eva shook her head. 'Please stay. It's nice to see people, and hear voices and…'

Rebecca took the phone from her. 'Let me dial the number for you.'

Eva nodded. It took her a few seconds to remember it and then it rolled off her tongue. It was answered in three rings.

'Nick,' she sobbed. 'It's me. I-I…'

'Eva, is that you?'

She nodded her head, unable to speak for the emotion from hearing his voice. For the first time, it sank in that her ordeal was over and she had survived.

'Eva?'

'It's me. I got out. I'm free.'

'Where are you?' Nick asked.

'Oh? I don't know.' She looked up at Rebecca. 'Where am I?'

'You're in Amison Gardens, Longton. Number 19.'

'I heard her,' Nick said. 'I'm coming.'

Eva cried as she realised the phone had been disconnected before she could speak to him again. But it was just as well, as an ambulance had arrived. Shortly after, there were three police cars and officers everywhere.

If Rebecca and Markus were shocked about the turn of events, they didn't say anything. It could almost restore Eva's faith in humanity. The complete opposite of what had happened to her in Alex's home. Here were two people who didn't know her – three if you counted Milly – who were going out of their way to help her. And yet all she wanted was the arms of one person to comfort her.

And suddenly there he was in the doorway.

'Eva,' he whispered, tears pouring down his face as he rushed over to her.

She fell into his arms and sobbed. It didn't matter that there were people around them. They faded into the distance and it was all about her and Nick. There was so much to say to him, to tell him and the police, but for now all she wanted was to be held.

Safe in his arms, where she belonged.

But she did have one thing to tell him that couldn't wait. She looked up at him, wiping the tears from her eyes.

'She'll be at the airport,' she said eventually. 'She told me she was catching a flight tonight.'

CHAPTER SEVENTY-NINE

Alex

I sit in Terminal One of the airport, thinking how my plan went wrong. For starters, I didn't estimate how strong Eva would be, even after all she's been through. And some friend Milly has turned out to be, letting me down at the last minute. I ripped up the letter I was going to leave out for when the police would rock up at the house. They were empty words now.

It hasn't all been bad. I didn't finish what I set out to do, but at least I will be notorious now. I laugh to myself as I think of all the neighbours in Amison Gardens, coming out to see what the commotion is all about.

As soon as Eva and Milly had escaped, I bandaged my hand, grabbed my bag and got out of the house. It would have been too risky to follow Eva and attack her, and besides, what would have been the point? My initial strategy had ended then, so I had to move quickly to plan B, which was to get out of the country as soon as possible. People will be looking for me.

I managed to get an earlier flight that is due to take off in just over an hour. Although scanning the crowds for police, I'm not concerned about getting caught. They will be all over the house for now, and talking to Eva and Milly. No one will know I'm here until it's too late.

I buy a sandwich and a drink and sit on a seat opposite WHSmith. I think I'll have a browse in there before I leave, perhaps pick up a couple of paperbacks to read on the flight. It's a shame I won't have Milly to discuss them with afterwards, but I will make new friends. This will be a fresh start for me.

Once I'm out of the country, I'm going to become Iris Stalward. Iris died five years ago. I like the name Iris, for now, anyway. If I'm to pull off another name change, I'll have to go under the radar for paperwork. It might be tricky to do it twice though. So while I decide where I'm going to settle, I'll think about what to do next. I might even go back to being Lara. I know Jude will like that.

Once I've bought two books, I glance up at the departure monitor to see that my flight is boarding at gate 21. I sling my holdall over my shoulder and march off. The walk is a long one. It's a happy one, too, as I listen to the excited prattle of holidaymakers. Kids going away with their parents, pulling tiny suitcases alongside them, dressed in colourful clothes.

That's how I should be by now. Taking children of my own away for a family break. My life could have been so different if it weren't for my mum meeting Ian.

I'm glad he's dead, my mum too. Now there's only me and Jude. It's all I need.

I catch a glimpse of the news on a widescreen TV. It's showing images of Eva coming out of a house in Amison Gardens. She's being shielded by Nick. I'm not impressed by that but there is nothing more I can do.

As I turn the corner into the departure lounge, I see a crowd of uniformed officers ahead. Shit! I put my head down and turn around, pushing my way back through the people starting to bunch behind me to form a queue. If I can blend in again, they might not spot me. I'll have to go to London by train and get out of the country some other way.

Thundering footsteps rush up at me, and I drop my belongings and run. Someone tackles me to the floor. I wrestle with the officers, but I'm no match for three of them.

I hear the handcuffs click into place, voices talking to me: words I've heard on TV programmes. They're reading me my rights.

They pull me to my feet, and I scream.

FEBRUARY 2020

CHAPTER EIGHTY

Stoke News

My Ten Days of Hell
Eva Farmer, Senior News Reporter
15 February 2020

On the day I escaped from Lara Dixon, it was her birthday. It would have been the birthday of her twin brother, Jude, had he not been murdered thirteen years earlier.

I was the fifth woman to be held by her, going under the alias of Alex. It had shocked me to the core to find out the person who abducted me was female. I'd interviewed three of the four women who had been taken before me and there had been no inkling. Of course, no one had seen Lara, so we were stereotyping from the small clues we were given.

We were beaten – hard, perhaps a woman wouldn't be capable of that.

We were held captive. How could a woman's maternal instincts allow herself to degrade us as she did?

We weren't sexually assaulted, although we all lived with that fear when we were in captivity. A man could have been impotent, using his powers in other ways.

Stephanie Harvey, Maxine Stallington and Alison Green were the three women who were released after being held for ten days respectively. Their hair had been hacked at, their nails cut and painted as black as the bruises that covered their bodies. They each had a number tattooed on their necks in order of their abductions. They were given the minimum of food and water and were held naked in a cellar.

Some of that happened to me too. I was given little to eat and drink, and I slept on a mattress with one sheet to cover me. I was dressed in a grey sweatshirt and jogging pants that weren't my own, and I had nothing on my feet. But I wasn't marked any way on my body except for the bruises.

Often I thought I was going to die. Sometimes I resigned myself to the fact that as the fourth woman hadn't come home, I would be the next to be killed.

They were acts of revenge that had gone too far. Because none of these victims, myself included, had ever harmed our captor.

As a child of ten, when her brother was murdered, Lara was taken into care. From that moment on, she chose to be invisible. Whether that was because she couldn't survive knowing what she'd been through, or if it was her coping mechanism, we'll never know.

After temporary foster care, Lara was taken to reside at Winterdale Children's Home. Louise Drayton, the residential manager at the time, recalled Lara as a shy girl who preferred to have her nose in a book rather than join in with the other children.

'But that was okay,' Louise told me. 'I saw a lot of children who would go into themselves. They were fearful, afraid. Everything they knew had changed, even if it wasn't a good environment to start with.

'After the trial, Lara was with us for a few months before she was fostered again. Until now, I'd always remembered her fondly. I don't know why she thought anyone didn't try to help her. We did, but she would smile and say everything was fine. I thought when she went to live away from the home, she would settle better, have more time to get to know a family, and for them to know her. But it seemed that wasn't the case.'

Stephanie Harvey, an ex-youth support worker, had met Lara when she was sixteen. 'She was ready to move into society and I found her a placement in a small room in a block for female teenagers with a live-in warden. I thought she was doing well, despite my initial concerns that she was a young-minded sixteen-year-old and there were support workers on hand during the day too.

'But then I'd had to leave the service quickly due to ill health and I couldn't go back. I've often wondered what happened to Lara. I would never have believed she was capable of something like this, though.'

Maxine Stallington, a retired social worker and the second woman to be abducted, remembered Lara as a quiet little girl too. 'She had trouble settling in with her second foster family,' Maxine said. 'I checked up on her regularly but I couldn't build up a bond with her. I don't think she trusted me because she feared I let her down over her brother's death. In a way, I had because I was unable to stop him from dying. His death still haunts me to this day.

'We hadn't long been alerted to the twins. A neighbour had phoned to express her concerns. I was unable to get into the property on several occasions before he died. My supervisor was applying for a court order, but the week before it came through, Jude was attacked and killed. I'm not sure I'll ever be able to forgive myself for what happened to that poor boy, and to Lara, but I knew I did all I could. We all did what we could. Often people blame the system, but sometimes it can only be the biological parents that must be held responsible. In this case, it was an evil partner too.'

Alison Green, the third woman to be abducted, fostered Lara when she was eleven. 'She would often stay in her room, preferring her own company to that of my husband and my two daughters. David and I fostered a lot of children, and our girls were always welcoming. But Lara didn't want to join in. It was her decision to go back to the children's home when she said she didn't want to be with us. I've never understood why. Now I realise she was crying out for help, but we were unable to get through to her just how much we could give her, if she'd only let us in. It's a tragedy what happened to her, but then again, none of us deserved what happened to us, especially Jillian Bradshaw and Maria Dixon.'

PC Jillian Bradshaw was a personal friend of mine. We met about five years ago. Her death hurt me deeply, and she didn't deserve to die. Jill was one of the kindest, most passionate officers I've known. Her almost stubborn streak often got her in trouble, as she stood her ground if she knew someone needed her assistance. She was like the proverbial dog with a bone if she knew she could help anyone who was under-represented and feeling let down.

During the time I was held, Lara told me she'd intended to release Jill on day ten. She claims to have given her too much of the drug she used to make us lucid. She'd administered this to the first three women, too, so she could release them, knowing they wouldn't recollect where they'd been, nor who she was.

Jillian never woke up. Whether Lara gave her too much of the drug deliberately or whether it was a genuine mistake, we'll never be sure. But it doesn't really matter because the world, and I, lost a good woman that day. Her body was dug up from the rear garden of the property where I was held.

But, regardless, by far the worst thing was that Jillian was a case of mistaken identity. She had never even met Lara.

With so little evidence, this was a hard case to crack. As Alex, Lara made it hard for the police to find her, despite their best efforts.

Staffordshire Police worked tirelessly to find myself and Lara, as well as the other women. Do I blame them for not tracking her down sooner? No. Lara was an IT expert. She hacked into my work's computer and had access to my emails. She knew everything I was working on, what the police were looking into – all the notes from the features I'd written. She kept herself hidden, purposely not making friends so that she could go unnoticed. She took a dead woman's identity and made it her own.

Was Lara Dixon an innocent victim or a callous abductor? In my opinion, she was definitely a victim, at first.

Maria Dixon, not long out of prison for the murder of ten-year-old Jude Dixon, was murdered by Lara after being beaten. Her internal injuries were severe and she was left to bleed to death. Her partner at the time, Ian Carrington, involved heavily in the murder of Lara's brother, Jude, was killed in prison, two years after being sentenced. The case was a brutal tale of child neglect and cruelty and both children suffered.

There will be a charity set up in Jillian Bradshaw's memory. The aim is to represent youngsters who get hurt through no fault of their own. We want children like Lara Dixon and her brother Jude to be the minority, and have a voice. We're hoping with our pooled experience we can help children in distress, provide someone for them to talk to, visit whenever things get bad at home.

This experience has without a doubt changed us too. We all have crosses to bear from our time in captivity. But every one of us tried to help Lara Dixon at some stage of her life.

CHAPTER EIGHTY-ONE

Eva

Coffee shops had always been Eva's favourite places. She'd often used them as resting spots between meetings, somewhere to catch up or work alone. Now, more than ever, she welcomed the noise around her. She didn't care about the clatter of cutlery, the chatter of people or the blast from the steamer on the coffee machine. She relished being among people again.

It was two days after Alex's trial had finished. It had been a tiring five weeks, and a painful six months since she'd escaped from Alex's house. Yet even after so long, the nightmares of her time in captivity were still coming.

Of course, Eva now knew for certain that all the things Alex had said about the four women she'd abducted had been false. It had been interesting, and disturbing, to learn what was true and what wasn't. A creation of Alex's imagination perhaps, to safeguard herself from the truth. Alex had been a quiet child, struggling to fit in with other people and preferring to stay in the background. But she had also been given the opportunities to live a normal life. It was unfortunate that her mind wasn't able to deal with it. After what happened to her, she thought everyone was out to get her. And who could blame her?

Back in 2006, the case of Witness1575 had been a tragic one. Even now it sent shivers down Eva's spine, if she thought about what Alex and her brother went through as children. How parents could ever treat their offspring in such a degrading manner was beyond her realm of thought. One day she would pen a book about it. It would be therapeutic for her to write about the ordeal, but for now it was too raw.

She hoped none of the abductees would be too damaged long-term as a result of Alex's actions. They were all safe now. The only harm would come from the mental anguish they'd been through. And something told her, their little group of four would be okay in the future. They would help each other to move on.

The women all bore the scars of what they had been through, regardless of whoever was coping and who wasn't. It was good to see how they'd had their tattoos covered. Maxine had chosen a rose, Alison had made hers into musical notes and there were the hearts she'd seen on Stephanie Harvey's neck.

The abducted women now shared an experience. Their WhatsApp group was going strong. It was hard to think how any of them would get over their traumas. They were linked by tragedy, bound by a case that had changed them all forever. Would they fight their way out of the darkness, the anxiety, the stress their experiences had left them with?

Eva had attended Jillian Bradshaw's funeral, once the body had been released. It had been a huge affair, upsetting but defining at the same time. A worthy send-off for a woman she had been honoured to call her friend.

In front of her now, Eva watched a mother attend to her young baby, settling him in his pram. Her hand instinctively went to her stomach. As she'd suspected at the time, she had been pregnant and miscarried. Now, it was early days again and she was three months pregnant. She and Nick had decided to wait until the birth to find out its sex, lovingly referring to it as whatever size of fruit it might be. At the moment it was a plum. If it was a boy, they were going to call it Aaron and if it was a girl, Nova.

It had been so emotional reuniting with Nick. After telling him everything, they seemed to be growing stronger every day. Now the news they were having a second chance at parenthood had cemented their love. Despite what had happened, Eva wouldn't let the experience define her.

Eva had made peace with her brother too. She'd met with Daniel and apologised for holding a grudge against him. No one but the two of them would ever know what had happened on the day that changed their lives forever. Eva hadn't even told Nick, and never would.

They'd talked it all through and were keeping in touch, if a little long between get-togethers at the moment. It was hard, but it felt right. He was divorced with a new partner and had a son who he saw regularly. Eva hoped to meet him one day too.

The coffee shop door opened and Eva looked up, waving at Milly as she came towards her. Since the incident, they'd been spending time together. It had helped them both to talk to one another.

Milly sat down across from her and smiled.

'How are you today, now that the trial is over?' Eva reached across the table and covered Milly's hand with her own.

'I'm… good.'

Last year had certainly taken its toll on them all but they'd got out alive. Eva hadn't been sure she would at one time, and she was certain that the other women would feel the same.

'You said you wanted to ask me something?' Milly said.

'Yes. How would you like to work with me when you finish school?'

Milly's eyes widened. 'Really?'

'Yes, really.'

But Eva watched as Milly's smile changed into a grimace.

'I can't.' Her shoulders dropped. 'It's not because I don't want to,' she added hastily. 'It's because I'm going to college.'

'I haven't explained myself properly.' Eva rolled her eyes. 'We were hoping you'd come and work for us once your exams are done this summer, paid – of course – and then when you go to college, perhaps you could work for us on day release?'

'Really?' she parroted. 'I would love to!'

Eva smiled. She'd hoped Milly would say yes, and she was looking forward to showing her the ropes. 'You can help out with the charity too.'

As she and Milly talked, Eva rested a hand on her stomach again. She would never forget the baby she'd lost, but was equally pleased that this one had been conceived when she'd been in better health. Who knew what damage the ten days she'd been through would have done to that first foetus? Now she was glad of the chance to give birth to a strong child.

New life all around.

CHAPTER EIGHTY-TWO

Alex

'Okay everyone. Let's start the session.'

I roll my eyes and look anywhere but at the counsellor. I am so bored with all these meetings. All they end up doing is getting patients agitated. Who on earth would think it's fun dredging up their past or talking about how damaging their addictions are? I mean, come on. No wonder no one speaks out.

'Alex, are you going to join in with our group session this morning? It would be lovely to hear a little from you again.'

Oh, it's my turn to be singled out today. I don't think so. I ignore him and look at my nails.

'Alex?' he persists.

'I don't have anything to say.'

'That doesn't normally stop you from butting in,' a woman sitting two seats away from me says.

I glare at her but she won't meet my eye. That's the thing with people in here. They say things, but then they back down because they don't want to suffer the repercussions. But I remember everything. When she's not looking, I'll spit in her food. I can't get my revenge in big ways, but I can do little annoying things that mount up over time. It's very refreshing.

I fold my arms and shake my head when the counsellor looks my way again. With resignation, he asks some other sucker the same thing.

I stare into space, anything to take me out of this room. I hate being here. No amount of group sessions, or one-to-one chats will make me feel any better.

Outside of this room, I behave myself – mostly. Everyone thinks I'm mad. I'm not because I knew exactly what I was doing. Those women wronged me, even though they won't admit it.

And I'm not telling anyone, because then they absolutely would think I'm crazy, but Jude is with me now. He keeps me company when I go back to my room. He's good to talk to, even though his thoughts are darker than mine. Of course I don't allow him to act anything out. I'm not that stupid.

No, we're just biding our time for when my release day comes. Doing as we're told. Letting people think we're not a threat to anyone.

It'll be a while, I know, but I will be out of here one day. I'll keep my nose clean. I'm not a threat to anyone while I'm in here. Because there are things I need to do, women I need to see again, like Eva and Milly. Women who wronged me. It wasn't supposed to finish like this.

If it weren't for Eva, I would be on a beach somewhere now. The police had no idea who I was, or where I was, until they caught me trying to catch a flight at the airport. I was so close to getting away with it. Once I'd got my revenge, I was willing to go back to normal life and no one would have been any the wiser. I'm not a serial killer, murdering people for kicks. I wanted retribution and, when it was over, I would have stopped. I just hadn't got to the end of my plan. Eva made certain of that.

I'm sure I'll be able to find Eva again. I expect she'll still be in Stoke. She might not even move home, even though I know her address. I can keep an eye on the newspaper, the bylines that she'll add her name to.

And that charity the women have formed. I mean, how more condescending can you get? Doing something to help others when none of them helped me.

Still, it will be different when I get out. No one can be invisible forever.

Not even me.

A LETTER FROM MEL

First of all, I want to say a huge thank you for choosing to read *Ten Days*. I hope you enjoyed getting to know Eva and Alex as much as I did. If you did enjoy it and want to keep up to date with all my latest releases, just sign up at the following link. Your email address will never be shared and you can unsubscribe at any time.

www.bookouture.com/mel-sherratt

Ten Days is the sixteenth crime novel I have published and yet it is probably the only book I've been wanting to write for many years. I have been fascinated by some of the research I've done around relationships between abductors and abductees, sadly in some cases over many years.

I also wanted the book to raise a lot of questions. Both Eva and Alex had troubled childhoods. Is it always nature versus nurture? Is there an evil streak in some people and not others? Could it be a sequence of events over a short period that makes someone crack, or a whole life of bad things happening to them? And how would we ever know after the event anyway? That's what makes it so interesting to write crime fiction. I hope I did this justice for you.

If you did enjoy *Ten Days*, I would be extremely grateful if you would write a short review. I'd love to hear what you think, and it can also help other readers discover one of my books for the first time. Or maybe you can recommend it to your friends and family.

Keep in touch,
Mel

MelSherrattauthor

@writermels

melsherratt.co.uk

ACKNOWLEDGEMENTS

I started my writing career in December 2011, after twelve years of rejection from publishers. To say I am grateful to the hundreds of thousands of readers who have invested their reading time in my books since then would be an enormous understatement.

Thank you to Team Bookouture, in particular to Peta, Kim, Noelle and Sarah. A special cheer must also go to Laura Deacon who has made this book a pleasure to write and work on. It's been fun to add the sparkle to my words with her expertise and encouragement and I hope there are many more books to come.

Particular thanks must go to the friends I am very lucky to have – Alison Niebiezczanski, Caroline Mitchell, Talli Roland, Louise Ross and Sharon Sant. Thanks for the long lunches, shopping trips, coffee and cake, Pimm's and cocktails and many, many book chats.

Finally I want to say a huge thank you to anyone who has read my books, sent me emails or messages, engaged with me on social media or come to see me at various events over the country. I've been genuinely blown away with all kinds of niceness and support from you all. I love what I do and hope you continue to enjoy my books. Your faith and support mean so much to me.

Likewise, my thanks go out to all the wonderful book bloggers and enthusiasts who have read my stories and taken the time out of their busy lives to write such amazing reviews. I am grateful to